Beauty

Mindi Meltz

Hidden Door Press
Mountain Home, NC

This is a work of fiction. There is no intended resemblance to any actual person or place.

Grateful acknowledgment is made for permission to reprint the following previously published material:

Excerpt from "To the Unseeable Animal" from *Collected Poems: 1957-1982* by Wendell Berry. Copyright © 1985 by Wendell Berry. Reprinted by permission of Wendell Berry and North Point Press, a division of Farrar, Straus and Giroux, LLC.

Excerpt from "Questions for the Stars" from *No Trace of the Gardener* by Yang Mu. Copyright © 1998 by Yale University. Reprinted by permission of Yale University Press.

Excerpt from *The Prophet* by Kahlil Gibran. Copyright © 1923 by Kahlil Gibran and renewed 1951 by Administrators C.T.A. of Kahlil Gibran Estate and Mary G. Gibran. Used by permission of Alfred A. Knopf, a division of Random House, Inc.

First Hidden Door Press edition published 2008.

Hidden Door Press
P.O. Box 833
Mountain Home, NC 28758

Publisher's Cataloging-In-Publication Data
(Prepared by The Donohue Group, Inc.)

Meltz, Mindi.
 Beauty / Mindi Meltz. -- 1st ed.

 p.; cm.

 ISBN: 978-0-9801773-9-8

1. Wildlife conservationists--Fiction. 2. Man-woman relationships--Fiction. 3. Human-animal relationships--Fiction. 4. Wildlife rescue--Fiction. I. Title.

PS3613.E39 B4 2008
813.6   2007910315

for the meadow, my first love

PROLOGUE

When I die, I'm going to become an animal.

I'm going to walk with the night like a dark lung inside me, like a lover pressed to my long belly.

Each footstep a question, to which the silent earth answers, each time, yes.

I want to be her: oily hair hooking the needles of the winter, ankles aching in the snow, narrow face nudged by a leaf, breathing.

I want the sleek of her leg, the way it fits in and out of the light.

When I die I want to be animal.

Hunger like a rhythmic question—constantly answered, constantly renewed. Wind like an ocean through the pines, and the movement inch by inch below: nuzzling, deft and urgent.

The hoof and the pinch of an oak leaf between the toes.

The hot presence of the world, and then the darkness. The red sharp bud and the red groove of the tongue.

Colors of scent now thick and brimming, now pale and frayed; now stained dark with blood, now sweet and open—hungry for my hunger. Now. Constantly now.

When I die I will be a deer, nosing the wind, becoming a darkness, and then gone.

"Come on, shy girl," he says over his shoulder.

I am moving somehow, but I don't know how, or what I am. I see the arched strides of his legs over the earth which, in the darkness, looks like water. I see his hands part the wet leaves which, in the moonlight, seem to cry out. His long back protrudes from the night and hurtles forward. His shoulders close like doors. His hair flutters slowly around his head like a fairy tale he doesn't know about. Nowhere on his body will he allow my desire to cling.

"Can you catch him?" he asks.

I shake my head. I can do nothing.

"Fine. Why did you come, then?" He lifts his fist so abruptly that the owl flurries out of the tree with a noise uncommon to it.

"But," I say, and the boy looks at me with an unreadable face I can now hardly remember kissing. "Maybe . . . be quieter?"

He says nothing—hands me the glove.

"No," I say, "I can't do it."

He continues to hold out the glove. I take it. I put it on my left hand. The owl is gone, like a fantasy in the darkness. There is only me and the boy. The usual things. The heat. The cold. The heart only a few feet away from mine, with just a little air and flesh between us—the only heart which could wake me from the cage of my dream.

The boy looks at me expectantly, at once asking and retreating. I see that he is also afraid, but even his fear he will not give me. I take a step forward and the owl's eyes appear, blinking, uninterested in love. I do not want to catch him. I want him to be free.

I raise my fist and, as always, he flies away, leaving me alone.

This is the way the memory comes, as I watch the deer pause vaguely by the side of the road and look back at me. It's been a year since I lived in that forest with you—that magical forest where the talons of owls and eagles could close around our fists.

I don't know if I'm remembering it correctly. But as I look at the deer I remember the immediacy of an animal's body brushing by me, like we belonged to the same life.

She stands perfectly still and looks back at me. My favorite animal. You used to say, *Deer are everywhere—there are too many of them. Why do you get so excited just to see one?*

And I am thinking of you again. Remembering what you felt like in the land where I knew you, where the whole forest was a riddle about love. I am trying to remember that moment, when everything changed. When something was finally captured, and something else finally released.

The deer flicks her tail, as if to signify her freedom. She turns her head and draws my attention into the limitless darkness behind her, and the darkness exhales the silent voices of the night. I remember living in the forest: the way the trees' breath softened my skin, drawing me down into luxurious shadows with a promise of rest—as if I could finally lie down in that sweet loam, decompose into pure sensation, give up my humanity completely.

Now I am standing on hard pavement, though the wind still falls through the pines in that way I remember, like sand.

I think, as I did then, that when I die I want to be an animal, so that I might gather the spaces of the forest into the contours of my body. So that I might know my place that perfectly—that everything I pass should only soften to the side a little, if it moves at all, and everything I touch should slip open like a flower.

And all my body should be a yielding downward, and a yielding into shadow, into roots, into the earth promising to meet me.

And I should know fear, but only that fear which draws me closer to another life.

Animal boy, I have been walking tonight along the street, into and among the lights of houses.

It is my mind that traps me here at the edge of the forest, looking in, trapped at the edge of infinity. I know that. I am thinking of you.

I try to focus on the animal who has paused here to browse between day and night. But the cold evening urges me toward home and the shelter of imagination. I am fascinated by a thought—what was it? How long since I've heard from you?

A long time, but it doesn't matter. You only wrote once, and you had nothing to say. You, the great speaker, wilderness teacher, lonely boy before the civilized crowd, cast down each written word with an awkward discomfort—like an alien thing. You hated the stillness of writing. You must always be moving, always flying away.

But still, in that other world—the impossible world, the writer's world—I was imagining you again, and imagining you were mine. Suppose you, in your animal life, existed to anchor me, the dreamer, to this world. Or suppose every day, and every night, I wanted you—wanted your movement, your sly prancing voice, your confident flirtation, your inelegant speech, your body rushing distractedly into the wild—and every day, every night, I had you. Suppose I wrote stories about having instead of stories about wanting.

But it would be the same perhaps, since I would still want, constantly, even while the want were fulfilled.

Because that is the nature of want.

This is the last glimpse I get of the deer. She dips her head lightly to kiss a leaf, like she might be able to forget me so easily. Tides of song and color are fading around her. The wind, unseen, combs the clamor of daytime into music.

I know that soon the darkness will rise, and the sky will fall into a blue like heaven and then deeper, into the marbled stone sleep of gods.

And then deeper into black nothing full of starlight from billions of years before.

But the deer will tiptoe onward, never looking up, her hunger lilting into the trees, because like you she doesn't care for the romance of stars. Like you she is so sweetly, simply alive.

How can I explain what it is, exactly, that reminds me of you? It's like a recurring dream—one I thought I'd conquered long ago—the way that animal face, expressionless, looks back at me now, asking me a question I'm afraid to answer. I feel the old stretching in my heart, not knowing what I am. Her senses search me, not understanding the kind of hunger that is mine.

That shy, ghostly, voiceless hunger.

And I stare like a predator for moments and moments, while I try to think of how to approach her—how to prove myself to the animal.

And while I am thinking—while I am trying, and failing, to accurately love the blurred song of her form, that whiskered vulnerability that is to me more powerful even than time and multitudes—she goes. She disappears so suddenly and well that I do not even see her absence until many moments have been lost.

I wake to the wonder of my solitude and—I have finally admitted to this, animal boy—I am still nothing but human. Still.

WINTER

*I hope there's an animal
somewhere that nobody
has ever seen.
And I hope nobody ever sees it.*

-Wendell Berry,
quoting his daughter

The boy is gone.

I ask the memories in my flesh, what is the story I wish to tell?

I ask my imperfections. I ask the hollow between my breasts, the stray white hair under my bellybutton, my too-skinny fingers, the dimples at the base of my spine. The mortal things—the things I can count on.

I remember one night when he began by touching me more gently, and his hand slowed to skim just the edge of my breast, as if one shape knew the other, and was curious at the knowing—curious at the familiarity, and the fondness of one shape for the other. Warm. But maybe I imagined that, and my uncertainty made my flesh tender, so that his fingers cut it like knives.

Still my body was so bright inside my cabin that night, like a meadow, and I, enchanted, asked him, Why is it so bright? And he said simply, Because the moon is full.

Maybe there was kindness in his voice. Maybe there was romance in his language. Maybe for one moment we saw one thing at the same time.

This isn't a story about opposites, though sometimes it begins to feel that way. But maybe coincidence is also an illusion, just a trick of the light that blurs two people together for an instant.

We were seeing each other, as we looked at each other, like concentric mirrors one inside the other inside the other, dazzling each other into infinity.

And for this, I have only words.

One

It was so easy, when I took that job in a far northern forest, to believe I wanted nothing but perfection. I didn't see him at first. I didn't even know I was hungry.

Loneliness did not yet have weight.

The place, perhaps, already spoke a certain language that I knew. It was just a wildlife research center in the middle of a wide, shapeless darkness on the map. I know nobody else, coming and staying for a season or two, and then going, would remember it the way I will tell it. But I must enter into my story in my own way.

This is because for me, in the beginning, there was no story.

I did not yet understand the meaning of darkness—darkness, from which a story is born.

For me, there were no names or even events yet.

There was just a cloak of white afternoon light over the roof of the humble cabin.

There was just that light dusting off a floating feather, and breaking onto the snow like pain.

There were the gesturing hands of two people who talked in the distance, unknowingly slowed by the yellow poignancy of the sun's last hours—and then skipping a beat, lost for a moment in brilliance.

There were the amazing shadows, climbing the trees. And the last light greasing the tree limbs gold, cupping faces in arcs of nostalgia.

People moved between the buildings. And the buildings lay still amidst the forest. And the forest was grand and soft-spoken and quietly infused with shimmering snow.

And here was my cabin; here was I. This much was real to me, I thought. I slept alone. I could not see the other cabins through the trees—where the researchers and educators lived. But I would pass them on my way to the larger building, which housed the dining hall and the kitchen, a couple of classrooms, and an office where data was stored.

Separate from these places was the old shed, where the wild captive animals were kept: the ones who were healing to be released, or who could never be healed—never be wild again.

On my first day I passed a man who sat outside his cabin, fixing some small metal contraption. His big frame hunched a little over the wooden table, over the smile that he offered me from his lined, unshaven face. The smile threw me a little, like an unexpected shaft of light. It had things in it I couldn't explain just then, and didn't have time to think about, because immediately he spoke and immediately there were answers required of me.

"You're new here," he said. "We haven't met. I'm not around much—usually out in the field—but you might see me now and then. So what do you do here? Are you in training?"

"Yes."

"With the rehab animals?"

"Yes."

I watched his hands as they twisted the wires of the thing he was holding—some kind of trap, I thought, for a small animal. I was watching his hands, thinking of raccoons.

A writer must trace the pathways of life in secret. She takes a job somewhere, joins a community if necessary, even takes up an identity—but with a secret motive.

"I see. Maybe you'll be involved in education then? I'm a researcher here. Right now I'm researching nest predation of . . ."

She is watching. She cannot say she is there to write, for then people would know her as a writer, and would watch her in her contemplation—would wonder at the worth of her mind, define her, question that timeless space she occupies in the rush of ordinary life.

". . . and is this the field you're planning to go into then? Wildlife rehab?"

"Uh . . . no. I mean, I'll just be feeding them. Or . . . whatever else is needed."

"Well, it sounds like you'll probably have extra time on your hands. You know if you ever want to come with me one day, I can show you what I'm doing out there . . ."

And it won't do to have them watch her, for they are clumsy in their watching. They watch with their eyes half-closed. They do not notice the light.

I realized he'd asked me a question again.

"I said, what sorts of jobs did you have before this one? Just curious."

"Oh. I don't know. Other . . . internships. Counting migrating whales. Watching wild horses . . . their behavior . . ."

The writer watches—watches everyone and everything, from the unseen places in her mind. She will live among them, even play the game, but the soul of her stands just on the outskirts . . .

"I see. And you weren't close enough, then? You want to get to know the animals a little more up close?" He laughed.

"Maybe."

The soul of her—the immortal part—keeps perfectly still . . . .

I thought I was there to watch the animals, and to find the original stories.

I had a sense even then that theirs were the ones that mattered—stories of hunger and pursuit, wanting and killing, nurturing and abandonment. The paths the animals wandered, and the wind in the hills wandering among them, and the waves and the light and the billowing leaves, and the restful earth under their hooves and the dreaming sky under their wings—these were the things people too often forgot.

Secretly, soundlessly, moving carefully in and out of the shadows, I would collect these stories.

This was my only purpose, I thought, and it seemed simple.

When I opened the door to the shed, I had to adjust to the cramped light. I was unaccustomed to the close smell of dead things and live things at once. I smelled suffering and growth. I smelled shit and hunger.

Ahead of me I saw the newly built room with reptiles on display. In the early morning it was blessedly empty of people, peaceful as a library in its shadows and sunny dust, with the old black rat snake sleeping in her big tank in the corner. To my right were the exam room and the room full of rats—the killing room. And here and there throughout the small building were the various unused spaces, indoor and outdoor, for the mammals that might be sent here in summer.

Through wire mesh screens directly to my left, silhouetted against the outdoors, I saw wings.

In the rats' room there was a chart that told how many ounces of meat each bird should receive, and how often. There was a list of tasks that needed to be completed, each morning and each evening. There were tanks and cages to be cleaned.

In the showroom, educators could lay the snakes out on tables and let them move freely. And there would be times when, from behind the foggy windows of the reptile tanks, I could watch the people as they filed in and leaned forward in amazement to see real animals being handled by humans—snakes wrapped around shoulders and necks, and great birds of prey perched on gloved fists.

And I would hear the broad careless noise of them, and be relieved by the walls and glass that hid me, and move as quietly as possible behind the tanks, doing my work. And if I ever heard a child ask suddenly, as the presenter waited for the talking to die down, "Who's back there? I saw somebody back there . . .," I would retreat for a moment, until they looked away.

I started my days out among the still molecules of winter air, flying, hoarding the freedom of my solitude.

There was light sugaring the winter forest, with its heavy boughs. And the stream carrying verses of light through the roots and under the ice to the lake, with the irony of light upon water—at once sharp and milky, neither transparent nor solid.

There was the wind carrying banners of light, fluid through the stiff trees, and rattling the frozen grasses over the marsh, and sweet for a moment along the rungs of the outdoor raptor cages, and flying far off there among the people.

And on the first day there was that man sitting at the wooden table outside his cabin, his lips moving over the comfortable nest of his beard, his big hand quick yet somehow restful as it moved the shining metal. Asking me my name and where I came from, or some other unimportant thing.

And inside myself, where it was safe, I thought, but could you ever see this day that I see? This day, made of nothing but light.

Have you gone to the window by your bed and sat under it with your head bowed, feeling with your eyes the muted passion of sunlight through glass, the ornate patterns tossed upon the floor through a place where the glass was cracked, like little fragmented deities from some lost and faraway heaven?

Have you seen the delicate ink shadow of your hand on a white page, more perfectly delineated than anything solid?

Have you seen that even the dust, revolving in a column of holy sun, was enough?

Have you seen the way the light makes paintings almost in color on the frozen lake, and meets the ice with its white swords shattering, and explodes in cold, unexpected places?

Have you seen it move on a person's face, silent and

unspeakably far, like a story being told on another continent? Have you seen those phrases from a language no one speaks anymore, that can no longer be pieced together into any sense? Like madness, but without the suffering. Like a symphony, but without sound—that light.

Such light, everywhere, dazzling. Sometimes it seemed I could not really look at objects, but only the wild and lawless designs of shadow-light—like a dream-story of things that played over the things themselves, mocking their reality. Glowing like that, like souls grown too large for their bodies.

But then I would come to the shed, where the animals were kept. I knew I had come here for the animals, but I didn't truly know why yet. And I would stop for a moment inside the doorway, while my eyes adjusted to the dimness of rooms which were not exactly dark, but not exactly light. I would lower my eyes as I listened to movement in the shape of cages: a language of shuffling, pained isolation that I could find no words for, but somehow knew.

TWO

Where did the boy begin in me?

My body remembers the smell of ice, and its contrast with the heat that bloomed upward from within. A snake of heat gliding up and down my spine, conducted by the cold.

The presence of the animals coming in and out of my consciousness like needles of sensation, each becoming part of the texture of a pain my body knew long before my mind did, long before I knew my body.

Was it love?

Or was it only this: volumes of darkness ballooning up from my belly—a tide of unexpected darkness, coming and coming and coming.

I sat in the dining hall and ate alone. I remember that wild and homey smell of the beams above me—wood that still remembers being trees. Trees mingled with sweat now—the wet casual scent of humans who had been cold inside their clothing, and now, baring their arms and faces to the indoors, were warm again. I remember the softness of the wooden table, like skin, as I dug designs in it with my fingernails and ignored the people near me, who were speaking of things.

I didn't mean to be alone, exactly. My aloneness was just something that happened—first inside me, and then all around me—and had always been happening.

And perhaps this is the beginning of the story: I remember thinking sometimes that I might die soon.

I thought, maybe I am having some premonition, and there will be an accident.

Because when you die, doesn't your soul go up in some puff of light? And just before it does, all the interactions of this worldly human world suddenly lose their meaning.

I could not bear the people near me going on as if they must constantly record mundane realities. I could not bear to hear even the names of the things that surrounded us—the names of lakes, the names of roads. I could not bear to hear people's commentaries on theorists or scientists. It was the way a comment was spoken—flippantly, and with complete disregard for the uneasy, long-surrendered passion that, one night in some individual soul's mind, created the form itself. Who was the man who wrote the article on the mating habits of deer? How did he feel when he watched them? Was he secretly excited? Was he lonely?

For a long time—before I'd even come to work there—I'd been witnessing this, the way everyone else seemed satisfied with ordinary conversation. But now it seemed I noticed even more the distance between me and the other people. I hardly felt human. And I knew I must be dying. It seemed that none of the daily words of living meant any more to me than they would mean to a person on her deathbed, perceiving only the light.

Now there was laughter at the table across from mine. I saw a boy my age lean back in his seat with comfortable pride, as if he'd just done something important with his words, whatever they were. His longish dark hair flashed against his face as he smiled, barely noticing himself before leaping into the next conversation. The others leaned in, laughing, like they never thought about anything. I stood up and left the building, emerging into the white air.

I had my own cabin at the wildlife center, close to the shed.

I had my own wood stove, with a fire I made every night humming inside it. Miniature explosions, like little gifts unwrapping, nudged each other in the huff of the fire-wind, all enclosed inside the iron. I loved the evening work of nurturing that fire and tending it for so long, like a flower, until it was strong enough to survive on its own.

Then I would wander around with a subtle smile on my face, feeling in the corners of my senses the oncoming warmth.

My cabin was small, one room. I had lanterns, poems, and paintings on my walls. There was a photo framed in birch, of me with my childhood friend, whom I hadn't seen in a long time. All things were in their right places. Sometimes I felt such a rush of gratitude upon looking at them, just because they were hanging there, where I had hung them. Because they had hung in so many places I had lived, and were always mine.

Into the night I would move in smaller and smaller circles

within the habits of my being, and finally lie down on my bed, in the center of my stillness.

From my black window the silence poured in, and I could see the moon and all the lands that the moonlight covered, and the mysterious plans the sky was making for tomorrow.

And I lay down with my notebook, bathed in a pool of the days' memories.

The kestrel in her cage, tiny and lovely and furious.
Her urgent eyes.

The Red-tailed Hawk, with her gentle fear, and the long grace laid out on her wings.
The still snakes in their tanks, watching, waiting.

(The people I met, faceless and nameless now, brandishing their cheery lines of greeting like friendly walls.)

Standing inside the cage of a falcon, and the surprise of wings around my head.
Silver trees rising from the lakeside ice, rotten, aching out into a sky flooded with ravens.

(The man's raccoon-like hands, turning, as if from far away.)

The long grasses of the marshland between the shed and the lake, hissing like paper dragons as I passed. A sound even below the level of silence, which only I could hear, and which could never, ever be spoken.

Black cherry twined into a mist of small green firs, and these turning gold with death. Each color like a knife in the whiteness, leaping upon my numb senses in the unbelievable cold.

And the lake itself: a great white page, drawn upon only occa-

sionally by the bony black stick-figures of dead trees, at once stark and intimate like the boom of my breath in my ears.

My own boots trudging alongside the tracks that wound out into the center of the lake in circular, senseless patterns. What was I hoping to find? As if the tracks would come to something . . .

(The boy's laughter, and I left the dining hall alone . . .)

I followed the rivers of prints where the deer once moved silently and en masse. I followed the little triangles of the squirrels' tight feet, leading repeatedly to trees.

I saw the tracks where coyotes came running together on the ice and met, and parted again, and went nowhere. I stood helplessly, seeing how I could only go so far, seeing how their feet had pressed into the thin layer of snow with more and more trust, until only their toes dashed against it, and then they flew.

The raptor woman was leaving her job in one week, and did not bother me with conversation while she trained me. We did not look at each other now; we both looked at the hawk, where it perched just at the level of our faces. She didn't hesitate. She lifted her arm into the air, so that the crook of her elbow was parallel to the floor, her shirt sleeve dangling behind her glove to reveal a sliver of wiry wrist. She pressed her fist into the crooked legs of the hawk. The hawk, its leg straps held tight in her hand, leaped lightly in place.

"Step up," she said, gently impatient, and pressed again. And the hawk, looking down abruptly as if surprised, stepped up onto her wrist—one, two. Quickly, she looped the leash around and hooked it to the straps.

I followed her as she walked into the other room, my heart rich with the colors, the textures, the reality of the hawk. I said nothing.

The woman held her arm next to the bar on the scale. Her bones were sleek and sharp, her hair bound tight and black against her head. When she looked at me, I was surprised. I heard the gritty, angular call of a crow come suddenly out of the thin sky beyond the windows.

"Roll your wrist backward when you want her to step off," she said.

The hawk stepped onto the bar, again looking down. The raptor woman held onto the leash and set the scale. The hawk, a creature meant for the sky to carry, weighed less than two pounds. The woman gestured with her head to the piece of paper on the wall. I looked at it with a quick flush of panic, up and down, and found the spot to write down the weight.

She placed her fist back under the hawk.

"When you want her to step back on, press against her legs and upward at the same time. And roll your wrist forward."

I said nothing.

The hawk said nothing.

"You try it," the raptor woman said, and handed me the glove.

Awareness flooded my face, my body. I took a step toward the hawk. Standing on the scale, it had nowhere to go. I took hold of the straps and lifted my fist, feeling the sudden physicality of the hawk's body through the leather, like my own belly. The hawk did not seem to notice me.

"Harder," said the raptor woman. "Press a little harder."

Nothing. I wasn't quite breathing.

"Go ahead. Press harder—it's okay."

I had to use force. I was forcing the hawk to step onto my wrist, so that her feet wouldn't get pushed out from under her. Now I understood. The hawk stepped up, and I felt the obligatory trust in her weight. The strength in my arm didn't feel like my own. The force was not mine.

But the hawk looked right at me and cried out.

A writer. Not animal, not human.

I had nothing to hold me.

I did not have that weight of homeness that animals carry in their bellies, that uninterrupted grip of their feet upon one terrain they understand. I did not have that ease of belonging with others of my kind.

I would not stay at the wildlife center. I would not stay anywhere.

But there was a wanting there that I did not know was going to hold me forever. It was the one thing I would be able to keep—that wanting.

It began in my throat—a sticky spot, where I did not say something. A string of voice like a wailing nerve between my mind and my body, twinged just so by silence.

I walked away that day, as I did so many days, into the snow and the light, leaving the hawk and the woman inside. I imagined being alone with the hawk, standing at the door to her cage. I was sorry about the cage. I was sorry about the leash in my hand. I imagined bowing my head to her, and her body flowing effortlessly—as graceful as the silence in her wings—onto my arm.

I walked until I felt certain I was alone, and then I turned onto a trail I had already discovered, and followed it to a place I thought no one would go. I entered a valley of wild sumac—fuzzy clumps of flowers blood red against the snow. Whenever I saw that color I felt a hot gratitude, and I ran down into it just to feel the rush of running, and when my feet sank so deep I could not go on I let the snow pull me down and anchor me to the ground. The light made the pine needles golden and translucent, and when I looked up it fell upon me through the broken clouds like rain.

Then I sat still, with the running still inside me. The great space of the winter all around me breathed with my breath. My eyes refocused. Down on the ground little ribbons of cat-like footprints meandered around me, and as my vision expanded outward in a wake of wider and wider circles I saw them running through the muddled deer paths and all over the hills. I had followed these fox tracks before. Today I followed them to a rotting log atop a hill. Along the log I saw a long nest of soft silver hair. And as I removed my glove to touch it, I saw small bones.

I touched one. I didn't mind. It was old and clean. A mated pair lived here, I imagined, and this was where they ate their meal together. Perhaps one brought it home to share with the other.

I sat there for a long time, feeling safe, feeling close to the foxes, wondering if this time I would see one—if I waited long enough, patiently enough, quietly enough.

But I didn't. And as I sat longer in that aloneness the sky dulled, and my mind went somewhere away from the foxes, and when it came back, the foxes, the red sumac, and the golden needles were somehow not enough. There was that thin thread, trembling, spanning the long distance between me and the dining hall full of people—and as my heart pulled against it, it stretched thinner, and my heart weighed heavier, and my mind blurred, and the sky was so big, and the light that tiptoed through the colors of winter could not touch me.

This happened sometimes. I did not yet know the importance of loneliness. I brushed it away and kept staring into the red flowers, waiting for the answer to a question I had not yet asked.

The rat's nose slips up close to the cold metal bar. She hesitates with the ugliness of the cold. The sour taste of the metal in her nose makes her snout twitch, and then she keeps twitching and catches up the familiar scents of death, rot, stillness, and hot moving fear—wriggling through her face and down her spine. Everything is familiar, constantly, and yet she never knows what it is. Has she ever known? The metal is familiar. She creeps along the metal as far as she can go, accustomed to the clumsy press of other bodies, each with its own urgent direction to nowhere. She comes to another dead end and her nose hits the cold metal again, now turning warmer here where a body leans against it: another rat half-sleeping, breathing heavily and stinking with the bodily intensity of life on the edge of death. Familiar body, familiar metal. She smells death all around, sliced through by an icy, terribly white stillness. All of this is familiar. Familiar too is the vague awareness of larger mammals passing through another, unattainable space, and the hands that might draw suddenly near, and even reach in and capture. That fear is so constant, so familiar.

But unfamiliar is the stillness of the warm mass that remains beyond the metal bars now, for several moments. A large mammal, neither approaching nor retreating. There is time in this creature to scent out the details—and there are scents that the rat doesn't really know, but almost remembers. Rich and fresh and complicated. They make her hungry and restless, but then she loses them in the din—the many weights of the familiar things. She moves around the cage again, checks everything again, and returns. She checks back with her nose: the creature is still there. What does it want? The signals seem unclear.

The pine snake notices a warm mass moving over her head. She checks the air with her tongue. Heavy heat—a large mammal. They come sometimes, like this. But this one confuses her. Its movement is slow and erratic. This animal must be prey: the snake can taste the fear smell, hot and cold at once. But it seems too big to be prey. And it moves strangely, like something injured, or something that does not know it can be seen.

The next day after I finished feeding the rats and the reptiles, I stood there for a while, watching the snake be still, and then I heard the raptor woman come in, and I went to find her.

In the empty showroom sat a carrying case with something in it. I came closer. The body inside seemed only a complex of vague scratchings, little thumps of feather against plastic—such an understatement of what could once have been wings and sky. But when I peered in, the head lowered instantly and peered back at me.

The eyes of an owl, especially when, in a dark space, the pupils fill them, do not seem to look quite into you. Instead they bulge like worlds in themselves, riveted globes, pounding in your own eyes like echoes. They are cold the way a dream would be cold, if you could touch it, no matter how warm and promising it may have seemed in your mind.

"He's blind in one eye," said the raptor woman, striding in, and the owl turned toward the sound and then bounced on his perch, lifting one foot and then the other—restless, I thought, at the sight of nothing but short plastic walls. "Great Horned Owl. Came from the rehab center in the city—we're going to keep him, because he'll never regain his sight."

That was it, I thought. The end of the owl's life as an owl. What would he be now?

The raptor woman bent down next to me and looked in. Her face was close to mine and I could smell her shampoo, like delicate chemical flowers. I noticed she had a scar over the bridge of her nose. I wondered where it came from. I wondered if she ever stood in front of the mirror and examined it from different angles, or tried to cover it up.

"Are you ready for your new home?" She spoke into the cage more loudly than I expected, as if speaking to a child. Her confidence surprised me as she opened the cage door and reached in with her gloved hand. I heard frantic beak-clacking and the swipe of cramped wings.

"Shhh," she said, and reached her other hand in. But as she pulled slowly out, and the owl's head emerged like a rough birth into the open space, he expanded suddenly into wings. Scrapings and clawings unfolded into the absolute silence of flight. The owl seemed unfazed by his blindness. He billowed through the dull air of the room and landed on a beam above us, smooth and graceful as a reflection.

The woman sighed, and we both stared up at him for a moment. I envied his certainty. He didn't know enough to wonder if we were good or evil, if we might be hiding in our eyes or our hands some hidden intention he couldn't fathom. He knew to fly away, and now to puff up his feathers and look big, and that was enough. He seemed a strange irony of confident terror, with his shifty lightness and his wide face, with his devilish feather-horns pressed back like an angry cat's ears.

"It might be worse to have two of us in here," the raptor woman said. "Why don't you go start measuring out the food for the other raptors, while I catch him."

But I want to be the one, I thought. *I want to be the one he trusts.* I recognized that silence. I would know what to do somehow. But I obeyed, because I did not know what to do, really, and it was easier to turn away.

That afternoon I followed the deer paths through the groves of Quaking Aspen. When I followed their paths I imagined I was one of them, with feet so gentle, and movement so unseen.

I followed the directionless light through silent pine forests, and through the soulful blowing grasses of the marsh. Once I came too near a main path, and heard the horrible clamor of too many people: a school group in sudden, unnatural colors through the trees, exclaiming at something. I turned the other way and disappeared as quickly as possible, not stopping until I came to the white and red valley of foxes.

Maybe today I would see them. I felt desperate somehow, my eyes skimming the stillness, hungering for a glimpse of something no one else could see.

Instead I saw boot prints down in the valley—my valley. The children's rude voices still echoed in my head, but I hurried down to the prints and examined them, first from the distance of my human height, and then from down low, like an animal, with my bare hands. The tracks were bigger than mine—a man's boots—and they were alone.

I stood up and leapt with my eyes from one print to another. Each one surprised me. They seemed more purposeful than my own path a few days ago, making a point at the fox trail and then veering off at an angle, returning at another point to check again and then moving off alone to some unknown destination. They had not lingered in wonder at the log or the bones, though they briefly paused. They had not stopped anywhere to rest.

I looked up toward where the tracks disappeared, through the valentine red of the winter flowers.

There were no other human tracks around, nor had I ever seen any here.

I stayed for a long moment, turning where I stood to follow with my eyes the looping script of that pathway, like a message written inside the very territory of my solitude.

I imagined his silence. I imagined him standing at the end of his tracks, looking back, and looking onward. I imagined him knowing something that only I knew.

I would never be able to name the importance of this moment—least of all to him. I know only that I felt I had in some way been secretly entered, and filled.

And that as soon as I felt this, I wanted more. And I continued to want more, without ever stopping.

Three

Nostalgia is the knowledge that you can never describe the texture of a memory in words.

It comes full-bodied in instants, and then goes, like the blink of a dream thrust upon your mind hastily—once, twice, three times—and then you wake. To the hazy, uncongealed present.

Spring came, in the end, with the bare arms and the relief of falling water.

But when I first feel the blink of that north forest memory, I feel my breath banging loud into the steel of cold stillness, and freezing onto my hair. I arrived there in the very center of winter, and winter was a huge and beastly angel in that vivid place, shaken intermittently from its stony sleep by the howl of the clenched ice on the lake—the bang of the air beneath it like fists on a drum, and the drum hollow with the silent world inside it.

My story begins inside this silence. Whatever they say about the colored thrill of summer and the rains of spring, winter is the season that haunts the writer. Winter allows her to be haunted.

Winter, where long ago stories were told around a flame, about the beginnings and ends of people.

Winter white, a blank page for the memories to write on.

In the winter of the North Forest every body was like an act of survival, contrasted with the merciless background of the snow. Every step contained the tension of ice—tense with the strain of a terrible tenderness I felt sure we must all buckle under in the end. But at the same time I knew it would never break—that grasp and pull of the ice and the soul—because it was a musical cadence, with the rhythm it thrummed between us.

I wish someone could remember with me that black march of the stark surviving things against the stillness. Every mark of life— every heedless stroll in the forest, every coat slung over a chair, every song sung breathily on a nervous walk home without a flashlight, every laugh in the headlights on a night off, every scratch of a chickadee's foot in the new snow, every pale stirring of aspen, every eye open in the predawn light, every hawk body over the marsh like an indent in the sky, every morning, every breath I would learn to take so cautiously to preserve for as long as possible the weight of his dark head on my chest before he woke and left me again—echoed.

At least to me.

He knocked on my door, about an hour before the first shade of sunset.

When I opened it I saw the boy I'd noticed one day in the dining hall, with the long hair shielding his overcast eyes and the mouth that laughed confidently without exactly smiling.

He seemed far somehow, as if he'd taken several steps back from the door after knocking. But I saw his face suddenly closer, as if I'd never seen it before, and it was instantly mesmerizing. It was that kind of face that is more shape than expression—bones underlining it in smooth, cool lines, like an animal's face, that does not brighten with a smile or contort with rage but remains vivid and eternal in its singular form. The only movement resembling emotion came from his shifting, snapping eyes whose light seemed somehow to approach and retreat at once.

All of this I saw in a moment, without needing any time at all.

"Hi, new girl," he said, and then immediately shifted his gaze away from my face, to cast it like quick and predatory points of light upon each basic facet of my surroundings: the room behind me, the bed, the emptiness.

I remember the hand he held out to shake mine, cracked and blunt and almost childlike, not graceful the way touch is supposed to be.

"Mind if I introduce myself?" he said. "You're so quiet. We see you sneaking around like a little mouse, not talking to anyone. Are you really shy, or what? Just talking to the animals all day?"

I felt the urge to answer him, but I shrank back instead. I felt like someone had called my name, but had said it incorrectly.

He nodded to the space behind me that was mine. "I used to live in this cabin, actually. It's the best one."

"It is?"

"Yeah, you get lots of privacy . . ." But now he seemed to reverse himself and move away again, and now he stepped back and sat down, straddling the bench of the little picnic table outside. The light was turning fickle as the sun moved to set: it shone suddenly with a manic gold passion on his face, then dulled and vanished, only to re-light its attention somewhere beyond us a moment later. His face remained unmoved.

"So what do you think of this place?" he asked.

"I don't know."

"Well," he said, "you'll get used to it. It's a pretty cool place, really." Which was what anyone would say, and meant nothing to me. But in that moment I had seen his eyes drop down my body, and I felt a sudden, instinctual confidence.

"What do you do here?" I asked him.

"Oh, I teach. Obnoxious fifth graders whose rich parents think they're giving their kids a well-rounded childhood by sending them out into the woods for a week."

"You don't like it?"

"Nah, it's alright, I guess."

I stared back at him urgently, trying to find a way to ask him why, then. Why was he here, who was he, and what did he really love? But without my asking, he said,

"I like it better when I'm out there alone. I'm a tracker. I need silence."

"What are you tracking?"

"Oh, I don't know. Anything. I used to be a hunter, actually."

I stared at him. His big boots. The relaxed spread of his legs. The fluency of his limbs in their warm wilderness clothing. His sharp nose hooking over his thin lips, like the beak of a raptor. A hunter—not a scientist. Hunter, I thought, amazed. Death. Killing. Like it was easy.

"Have you ever been to that valley where the fox dens are?" I asked, my voice suddenly caught in a near-whisper. "Where the sumac is in bloom?"

He laughed at me. "There's lots of valleys," he said, "and lots of foxes. You should get out more."

I looked down, embarrassed. His voice softened.

"I've been everywhere," he said. And then, "What about you? You haven't worked much in a setting like this, I guess?"

What had given me away? "No," I said, "I mean, yeah, I have. I've done fieldwork before. But I wasn't good at it." This came out somehow. I wanted, suddenly, to talk.

"No?"

"No, I mean, well I couldn't remember the names of things.

I loved being out there. I loved it. But I . . . I don't know. I'd get lost."

"So now you're locking yourself up in the shed with the caged animals?"

The wind blew a little around me. I felt that subtle desperation, at once familiar and new. "I do like it here," I said. "But I'm . . . I'm not like the other people here. It's . . . hard to explain."

"So you get lost in the woods . . ." he mused, and I pictured him alone out there, going everywhere, finding what I was looking for, whatever it was. "Are you afraid of the dark?"

Yes, I thought, but I said, "I love the night," which was also true.

"Well then we're going on a night hike," he said. "Meet me in the staff lounge after dinner."

And I didn't mind this demand he made of me, because I felt a sudden, intoxicating joy.

Beauty is also an emotion. There is an emotion which is precisely expressed by the color of the sky before blackness, when, in summer, the thrushes sing. It's that color you can never describe again, no matter how faithfully the memories play in your mind.

Maybe I write for the sake of metaphor. Coincidence. These strange associations: the hang of his shoulders as he shrugged his invitation, the white burden of snow drooping from the branches like loosening muscles, the falling of day into night.

The patterns repeated: repeated in faces, in sunlight-on-water, wind-through-trees, or fire, or two bodies slung haphazardly together into the contours of sleep.

Now there was this time to wait, this time where I was thinking of him. No, not thinking of him exactly, but feeling him. The heat of him in my chest, growing. The heat I hadn't even been aware of until after he was gone.

Does he think of it? I needed to know. *What happens for this casual boy, in the moments between anticipation and fulfillment?*

The gazes of people trap me.

I had entered the room to find the boy, and for no other reason. But their eyes all turned on me as if my entrance were some kind of statement that I had to defend. A moment before, alone and full of hope, I was like a poem I knew by heart. But now, among people, I broke into pieces, and felt my mind scurrying around the room trying to find them, swearing I had a voice here somewhere. But in the end I just gave up and waited for the gazes to drop again, and cringed at the questions.

"Where are you from?"

"Where did you go to school? What did you study?"

"Ever been this far north before? How do you like this weather?"

"How's it going so far with the animals—are you learning much? Going to teach any classes?"

No, no thank you, I said, panicking in a sea of small talk, floundering for a glimpse of the boy, and when I found him he was talking, laughing, part of every conversation, everywhere.

When the animal boy walked beside me, I didn't think. I tried to match his confident pace and I knelt beside him when he showed me the stories of animals written in the winter. He squatted by a log and pointed to the square of the weasel's four footprints. Different than a hare's or a squirrel's.

"See," he said, "a weasel runs like this, like an inchworm. Some species of weasel always jump over logs, and some species always go under them."

He showed me the fish scale droppings of the otter, like piles of gleaming mica, and her musky channels through the snow bank, and the tracks of her webbed feet and even the tracks of her whiskers against the bank where she sniffed at the ground.

I imagined her digging for sleeping frogs deep inside the dream of the water, digging beneath the ice where the mud was still fleshy and alive, using her sense of touch to survive. The only sound was the hiss of the boy's jacket against itself as he shifted to the other knee and then stood, shoving his hands inside his pockets. He kicked with his heel toward the weasel tracks.

"He stopped there," he told me, " to listen to something under the snow."

"Under the snow?"

"Lots of things hide under there. There's a whole layer of air under the snow where they spend the winter."

"A whole other realm . . ." I murmured.

And he said enthusiastically, "Yeah—exactly," like he was teaching a group of kids, not knowing what it meant to me to imagine this, or to wonder what he thought about it—this secret layer where small things survived.

"You want to walk out on the lake?" he asked.

In the twilight the winter had a kind of howling stillness, and through it I experienced his smooth sharp wake as we walked, like the unswerving motion of an arrow. He felt dark—and alive in the instinctual way that night is alive. His jaw angled off dramatically like a cliff, and I wanted to touch it. His grin, cold and gripping as he looked over at me with his wet black eyes, startled me because of the flirtation—because he seemed, already, to want the closeness I suddenly needed, and yet from so far away.

When we stood facing each other way out on the frozen lake, armored with the round clumsy bluff of our winter clothing, he began asking me the questions that people ask. It was an easy curiosity in him, to know anyone.

But how could I describe the world I knew to him? How could I tell him how moments like these moved me, when the wind rung like broken glass in the trees, and even the dying sunlight billowed and tumbled—a wayward, fickle film of gold that would skip, at any moment, off the world entirely?

And how the snow's white was iron cold, and later—wonderfully, heroically—would be glazed in blue. Oh there is nothing I want more than that shade of blue the snow takes in the evening—a color in which I should never again be ugly, and never again disappointed.

"So you're the raptor girl now," he said.

"I'm better with animals," I said. "I could never do what you do. Teaching scares me."

But why did I have to always begin that way? With something I could not do in this world. I had worked in wild places, watching animals from a distance. I got to work alone, and I imagined that the animals knew me, deep in their peaceful psyches, as they moved and lived in the easy circle of my binoculars. How could I explain why I'd come to this place now, a place where I would spend all day with wounded animals trapped inside a room? I still wanted to be alone with the animals, but I wasn't good at those private jobs out in the wilderness after all, navigating forests and fields on my own. Animals would see me before I saw them, and disappear.

Now I had only to walk along a trail to the shed and they

were there, always in the same places, fluffing their broken wings and staring straight back at me. But these animals knew something strange about life. They knew about a pain that outlived life. They knew an intense separation from life that the wild animals had never known.

"Well," the boy said carelessly, "Everyone has insecurities." He tossed the words over my shoulder, and it was as if he said, "I have nothing to fear." It was as if he did not care at all whether I saw the strength of his voice go marching over my shoulder, or whether I just let it go by.

But he did care. He needed me to see it. Because I am the one who carries beauty.

He told me boastfully then about how he got the kids lost one time, but he wasn't worried. One girl was crying, he laughed, but he didn't let on that he was lost. And they got back okay, of course.

I fell under the spell of him. He was a tracker half of the time and a teacher the other half—a loner and an entertainer at once—and bold in both. I imagined him wandering, like an animal, knowing exactly where to go. I could never find my way like that.

"Watch out for those raptors, though," he said. "They'll eat your face off if you let them."

I looked wistfully at the bare corners of his face. "Not yours."

He laughed at my seriousness. "Oh, I don't spend much time in the rehab building. Those animals don't like me much."

"Why?"

"I don't know. It's not really my thing."

"What isn't?"

"Turning wild animals into pets."

"But that's not the point."

"All you girly animal rights activists trying to save every little baby that falls out of its nest. They're *supposed* to die."

The darkness began to sift into the trees. I think I missed

the blue time entirely. We were standing on the water, and the water was solid. I looked at him, confused.

"What does it have to do with girls?"

"You know, women want to nurture things. They get all emotional."

His body stood stolidly and faced mine, not moving much except to press his hands deeper into his pockets. There was something in him, not his confident body, that shifted and fluttered. Something he could not see, I thought, that made him uneasy.

"What do you mean?" I said. "You don't have any emotions?"

"Of course, sure . . . I have emotions."

"So?"

"So people think it's not okay for an animal to die. Everything dies."

"But those raptors wouldn't all have died naturally. A lot of them were hit by cars or hurt by people somehow."

"I just don't like working with things in cages."

"But . . . you use those raptors to teach classes with."

"Yeah, but only because people are too lazy to go into the wild themselves. They have to have everything brought into a room for them like it's on TV."

I looked at him, fascinated. He was right. Those raptors we half-healed and kept, with their unnaturally prolonged lives— they weren't even real. This was what bothered me, exactly.

"Don't get so worked up," he laughed. "I'm sure you'll have fun taking care of the raptors."

"But I was just thinking . . . I agree with you," I said helplessly. I wanted him to know it. I wanted him to understand our connection.

"Great," he said carelessly, looking to his left, into the forest.

I love the wild too, I wanted to explain. *I'm a writer.* But he wouldn't understand. Some things should not be spoken, I told myself.

"Look, did you see that? A fox," he said. I turned quickly, irritated that he'd ignored my silence and at the same time seen something I so wanted to see. I was losing myself. How did that happen so quickly, with only a few spoken words?

We kept standing there in the sunset. I didn't see the fox. All I could see was the boy's body in front of mine. On some winter nights the white-laden forest never truly gets dark, but only softer. It only dims and fades together, so that all shapes become fuzzier, in a way that would make you laugh if it weren't for the grandeur of the silence. All you can sense is the warmth of another body, in its tremendous contrast to the vast and eternal cold.

My feet scuffed the ice with an excess of nervous energy, making confused tracks in the skin of snow that no animal would ever make.

And I thought about how easily a setting of ice and stars makes you want to hold someone.

He thought about something else. I still don't know what it was. Maybe sex. Maybe nothing.

Whiteness gathered and shone in the increasing dimness—white snow pressing into whiteness—until all my little thoughts became suffused with whiteness. The white trailed all over the air, and then the white turned pink, and the sunset ached upward through the mud reflections in the distance, pink and gold. This palest, earthen pink began in the halo of the lake and then gradually revealed itself in every dimple of the forest's body.

And the glass layers of the lake's horizon sank in and out of the night mist, white and pink and white, like shades of unattainable bliss.

The night helps things. It gathers things together that might not have made sense, and gently merges them.

Even civilization I can almost bear at night. Dressed in darkness it is almost lovely. But still the wind feels empty. It flails helplessly over the pavement, that toneless infinity—no leaves to crumble in ecstasy under its touch, no thickets to draw it close and soothe its fervor, no curves to shape its dance, no life to interact, to be kissed by it, to tremble against it. It flails about in boredom, like a mind without focus, a mind without body.

In the whole grand brilliant civilized world, with all its excitement and strobe lights and sleek plastic bodies, I can never find again the precious loneliness I discovered that year in a faraway winter forest. That loneliness where each human life is so singular and dazzling, where the warmth of a single touch is the answer to everything. I have searched the human world for that loneliness—that vivid, sparse loneliness—but I have found only the loneliness of empty pavement, the loneliness of a thousand people.

Sometimes when I come home these days, before I turn on the light, I can't remember at first where I am. Tonight I stand very still, thinking: I could be anywhere. In that cabin, for example, in that forest where you lived. Where I could be hurt that way. Where my heart grew up from the center of the room, and shuddered its thorny limbs against the ceiling at night, and wept a shining ivy, and sunned itself in a desire so bright that all I can remember, as I tear through reams of nostalgia in search of that actual boy of flesh, is the color of desire, over all my walls, over all my night and my room, as I waited for you to come in.

We had sex inside my own cabin that first night, by a fire he made. I remember the wings the firelight made on the wall.

I remember the slow, almost imperceptible crumpling onto the bed and the falling of clothes: the downward motions.

First there was the excuse of his needing to look inside this cabin where he used to live. He was curious, of course. He'd lived here for almost a year. I invited him in and waited for him to look at all the pieces of me arranged carefully on its walls. He didn't say anything. His eyes moved stubbornly over my arrangements and seemed preoccupied with something else.

I sat down on my bed and watched him build me a fire, without asking.

I remember his low smoky voice as he tried to seduce me, not realizing that he didn't have to—and the ridiculous game of his charm. The strength he paraded seemed impossible. He talked briefly of girls and boys. He said, "Girls are crazy," and looked down and grinned. He said, "I want a girl who knows what she wants." He said, "I want a girl who can take care of herself, who doesn't need me to lean on."

That was me. I knew what I wanted. I didn't really need anyone. I was a writer. I just needed this: a leaf of beauty in the night, and a single, perfect moment's connection. I sat by him, wondering about his body, waiting hungrily for the end of conversations—for the cliff we would come to, and the long poetic fall.

I felt I had always wanted this boy, who was like an animal without even knowing it. I had been seeking him all along in the spiraling tracks of the animals on the ice, never reaching him because he was always moving, like a fire—as if the black night itself were a fire, independent and free, taking the whole world as if the whole world were easy.

When the moment came, it took only a moment. After all there is a quieter point within me, the cold white point of knowing in the center of my breastbone, where I saw his approach and retreat, and we both knew what was happening.

Sometimes I think this point of knowing is my soul. But I'm not sure.

I let him play the game but I was not playing it with him. I was only waiting. For me there was only, at this time, the color of blue that the snow takes in the evening, and the dim outline of his jaw in the warm darkness. There was nothing to distract me from this need. I didn't have to do anything. I just let myself be carried.

I knew that part of me was immortal. And for the immortal there are no stakes; there is nothing to lose.

But when he kissed me without resistance, and then so quickly entered, I felt I had missed something. His touch seemed a natural part of the conversation. We were lying down anyway by this time. He kissed me as a boy kisses a girl, pressed his palm along the length of my thigh because it was the motion of a boy upon a girl.

But I did not have him. It was all over and I was back again, waiting indefinitely on the edge of the cliff—alone and wingless.

It ended so fast that I realized how he had concealed his excitement—and how I had not really captured him. I had not tasted the sweet smoke in his voice or the ease of his stride. I wanted that wild presence inside him—I wanted to touch the aloneness I saw there that made me know he could have walked away into the night, as if carefree, had I been able to say no.

We stood awkwardly at the door. My cabin would never be the same to me. It was like a once simple object now hung with dangerous shadows and hypnotic light.

"Well, goodnight," he said.

I tried to hug him, but it didn't work somehow. He laughed nervously. It was too intimate; even cushioned again by all his layers of fleece and wool and down, the hug was too intimate. In our whole evening of naked touching, sweat mingling, we had not actually hugged.

So he stopped my hug with a kiss, and said again, "Goodnight," as if to reaffirm the goodbye.

This was the only kind of nakedness we would have, then: the kind that revealed nothing.

Thereafter, if I wanted him, I would have to stalk him sideways, averting my eyes, like stalking a predator.

Winter is the writer's season. Winter is a celebration of long-ing—of the brittle, shiny absence of touch. The animals suffer through it. It is not a place for the body.

It makes you lean ever so slightly, tempted, into death.

Four

I thought of the raptors constantly.

I thought of their stillness.
I thought of their tiny flights from one perch to the next—
and no further. Their cages were big enough for birds who cannot fly, or who should not fly because they have suffered some
injury which would make flying unsound.

I keep remembering that forest, as if the people who moved
me are frozen there, as if I could return to them—and most of
all the boy, with his heat and his freedom. But they have all left
to follow their different lives.

The only ones I could return to, if ever I could return, are
the birds, who cannot go. Who are ghosts. Whose lives were
drawn out beyond death, and who live on without possibility,
without story.

They perch there still, in the same cages, with the same furious fear in their eyes.

My first day alone there I had not yet learned how to kill the rats, so the woman had done it for me, and left containers full of tiny body parts in the refrigerator.

I walked along the indoor edge of the cages, blissful with relief in the warm ring of my aloneness. Inside that ring appeared another being: a tiny blind Screech Owl. He sat in a corner of the darkness, at the very end of his perch, waiting for things he could not control—his eyes permanently frozen in a fog of fear.

How could he live, I wondered, knowing he should not be able to, even for an instant? Surely he must feel it in every weightless bone—the prey that he ought to be, as a small blind thing.

And I thought that this moment of silence, of contemplative sympathy, would earn me something. But as soon as I moved he hurtled into the air, banging the mesh walls in search of a new perch, until finally he clung to the wire itself with his dry wormy toes, slowly rolling his head around in search of my sound. I took another step, hating my humanness, and opened the cage door, and spoke.

My voice took my breath away. He tore himself into the air again, first flinging his head back, dead eyes huge and skyward, as if succumbing to some quaint anguish.

So I just dropped the meat on his perch and scuttled out again, then closed the door and watched him from a distance. With his feet he felt his way along the perch to the food, creeping with head pinched back and stiff with anxiety, oblivious to my longing for trust.

Could I be quieter, then? Gentler? Could I be invisible?

I went outside to where the bald eagle lived, in his outdoor cage. He paced like a tiger because he could not fly at all. He greeted me head-on, glaring, crying his tiny, stuttering whinny. When he approached me boldly, my own fear wriggled in my throat like the live fish I tossed to him.

His eyes were like statues, and their movement as unexpected and as eerie. The black balls rolled so slowly downward, as he focused them like cold holes on his prey. His every step came brutally somehow, his feet a ribbed chalky leather, his head a kingly crown.

But he did not eat yet. He looked at me with the solid suns of his eyes, and then back at the fish dying in his grasp, and then back at me. And I saw that when people question the mental intelligence of animals, they are asking the wrong question.

He feared me too, then, even if only vaguely. I could not give up. I wanted to offer him something I thought the boy and all his scientific colleagues could never offer him: my love.

But all the raptors feared me. And not that day, nor for a long time after, did I really understand that nothing I could ever do would relieve that fear.

Nothing I could ever do would make me something other than what was feared.

Gradually I had to learn who people were. Here were two teaching interns who worked with school groups and gave tours to adults. Here was a man who studied small mammals, and another who studied birds. And here was the boy—whose body still moved hot and close in my memory. Who seemed to be involved in every project, who could do anything.

I learned my way around the Center. Here was the shed where the canoes were kept, for educational groups who went out to look at the loons and other waterfowl in summer. Here was the office where researchers sat typing their reports and conversing lightly, and where the boy stood among them, telling his boastful tracking stories and his crude jokes amidst friendly laughter, glancing over briefly now but perhaps pretending he had not seen me.

Here was the staff lounge where people socialized in the evenings sometimes, and here lay the string of cabins along the long trail into the dark woods. Here, at the end of that trail, was a small yurt—a temporary structure, like a big round tipi, invented by some nomadic people long ago. It sat in a clearing alone by the lake, made only for one person to sleep in, and that one person was the boy.

Here was the forest for miles in any direction, and the lake containing several layers of inconceivable darkness over a long-frozen earth.

In Alaska, the boy would tell us, eagles were like gulls. They were everywhere. He'd hiked around Alaska with a girl. He didn't talk about the girl, but he talked about Alaska, and all the rarer birds, and the names of the cold mountains. His loud voice was part of every conversation. He could hold the bald eagle on his fist with the leather straps, and he could hold all the other birds too, and hold them down to trim their unused talons. He named all the songbirds. He knew how to track the animals. He knew the different shapes of their scat and their tracks at different times of the year. He knew the life cycles of all the hungry mammals slinking under and over the snow. He knew how to teach all the raptor programs, and most of the other classes, and he knew how to fake the ones he didn't. He knew the names of the stars and the constellations, and the chart of the sky. If someone asked him if he was ever wrong, he would laugh at himself, but not really, and grin seductively, and say No. He knew how to make the little girls in the school groups giggle, how to impress them in his presentations by saying gross things about the owl squeezing the rabbit's guts out.

"It's time you learned how to kill," he laughed, not looking at me, and I was still standing there in the doorway to the rat room with surprise confusing me, and realizing that even this he knew. This place too—the raptors, the rats, the cages he hated—was within the scope of his knowing and the terrain of his days. He was not torn apart by this; he did not stand in front of the cages and wonder, his heart twisting about uncomfortably in his human body. He was moving now, and always moving.

"She's busy or something this morning," he said, apparently in response to the question in my stillness, "so I'm supposed to show you how to gas the rats."

I felt a lurch in my heart, that it would happen like this, all of the sudden. I watched his ugly hands in their suave and childish motion, and listened to his quick instruction. With a scissor he gutted and cut the bodies of those who'd already been killed, and then deftly weighed the parts—gloppy, one-eyed, ragged—in containers, and added the intestines to a bucket of intestines all coiled and clumped like a brain in the freezer. Then he picked out the rats to be killed today. I watched his untroubled body moving around me, intent and eager, alive and rushing with solitude.

I thought it was not the rats' deaths but their lives that seemed wrong.

They twisted in their cages like fat stranded fish. They examined the same corners repeatedly all day. Even when they sat still, pressing sociably against one another, they shook with movement. Three rats to a one-foot-square cage, with rat pellets lain on top.

Rats are smart. They form societies and cliques. They go to war with each other. They love their friends, and are curious. They like varied diets.

The killing room was the same as the living room for the rats, and their sense of smell is much better than ours.

The air was pallid and rank, and the refrigerator hummed, and the light that snapped open the windowless darkness in a timed dawn, every morning, was dull and cottony.

"I feel sorry for them," I said daringly.

"Yeah," he said abstractly, turning on the gas.

The raptor woman came in, just as the boy turned to me and said "Hi!" with a disembodied rat head as a puppet. Then he made a scary dead-rat-head monster noise at her.

"Be nice," she said, and then to me, "Just ignore him."

I smiled in what I hoped was a casual way, hating my own silence.

"Come on, are you done being an idiot? Come in here, I want your opinion on something . . ." and she walked into the other room talking about an infection around the new owl's eye. I watched the submission in his walk as he turned and followed her, and I felt a heat shake me like some great perverse hand had just slid through me without regard for the boundaries of my body. I could feel him inside me and I wanted to know if he would ever touch me again. Did he not think of it?

Through the doorway I could see him pass through the classroom and past the black rat snake's tank, and I watched her whip suddenly into a hot sling of motion, rearing up against the glass with a hiss. I smiled a little to see the boy jump.

"Goddammit," he said, letting his breath out, "Why does that fucking snake hate me? She never hisses at anyone else." And he stood there for a moment and looked at her with a kind of thoughtful frustration that filled me with longing.

But then their voices faded and I relaxed to know I was alone. Behind me I heard the din of urgent scrapings like a monotony. Bumping about in those cages, the rats looked like gross puppets already. They looked prepackaged for death.

But nothing is ready for death, I thought, until it has lived. And I could feel the tension in the muscles around my spine, like the voice of every unspoken thing coiled tight along its length, as I exhaled with the relief of being alone in the room again—of no longer having to fit myself inside people's eyes and people's minds.

Sometimes I think I am not really alive except when I am alone.

I do not even miss my own life, or remember that I live it, until I am suddenly alone again, and seem just then to begin breathing.

Here is my own self dancing, following itself into fields at night where the deer go, able to believe that nothing is more necessary than a line of thin pines in front of the moon over dark water, and the ruff of clouds above it, and the moon a pinwheel, that seems to hold my own face and all the desire of my heart's eyes within it.

Here flies the downy wind traced by the long flapping of my white hands like moths while I watch them, mesmerized, and here I dance for a moment like I no longer need worry about my humanness in this world, watching myself free of being watched.

Some nights, as I returned from the shed, it was too dark to see anything anywhere but the faintest white blush of snow. On those walks the whole world opened to my soft self gliding through the tissue of the darkness. Nothing challenged me; the darkness eclipsed everything I could have feared. My crazed mind sat still for once, like a child caught by wonder, bouncing gently in a fairy tale carriage that the animal of my body led home.

And what home anyway? I had just come, and would leave in a few months, and move on, and then move again.

So why, late that night on my way to feed the owls, did I take a longer route to the shed, and why when I passed by the lounge did I linger there, as if hoping to see him? I didn't see him, but I heard his voice inside.

I heard, "See you later, man" and "Goodnight," and saw someone not him walk out of the building and toward me along the snow-lit path. I stood there before the building, having no purpose there that I could admit to, and not knowing how to make one up.

"Beautiful night," the other man said amiably, as if everything were normal, as if I were not suddenly crippled by desire and dread, my chest hollowed out like a burning house. I pretended I had never meant to pause there—that I was headed onward, in the other direction.

I started running through the white night.

I ran, and the snow haloed the darkness, and I was alone, and okay. Young firs, dispersed about the meadows, took whisked and sudden forms. They called me into them with a wildness more utter than fear, so alive in the silence I thought they would spring upon me in a mad dance.

The shadows seemed to shout. The stars bled. I danced along the trail and all the way out to the dirt road, spinning, hearing my hard breath bounce before me in the cold. Desire pumped life into my body like an organ in itself, and then it spread smoothly out into the ring of night around me like a wave when I stopped.

Woman in the trees, lapped by tongues of the night. Eyes upheld to the stars. Her white skin turning inward to its own shadow. The lisp of hair against her cheek. Her hips hot through the down, through the restless sliding of cloth. Hair sweat-edged, damp, not yet frozen. Fleshy night. Cold and silver. A night like knives and kisses.

The winter darkness turns to butterflies. The trees unfold. The sky sinks into oblivion, she falls to her knees. Tell me the secrets. Tell me your dreams, in no order.

I watched myself. I am always watching.

As if hoping that finally, magically, I will become the poem I'm writing. As if I will suddenly begin to know the story I belong to.

But when the desire subsided the fear returned. Was it the darkness, or the things inside the darkness, or the things inside my mind? I sang a little song to hold the fear down. I quickened my pace to the shed. Inside, I whipped around to close the door and turn the light on in one motion. The mundane scuff of my shoes on the cement floor comforted me.

I stood before the Great Horned Owl's cage.

An owl flies silently. I don't mean that he flies very quietly. I mean that he is there, and then not.

And then he is looking at you from the far end of the darkness. His eyes are too big and throbbing for flesh of this world. Their vision pulses against your own. You are at once still and restless. You look into them and feel that you might never find peace.

He stared at me; he hissed. I wanted him to know my respect. But my stillness and wonder there, staring back, only tensed him. In the wild an alert animal is only completely still when in fear or in ambush. What did he know of my thinking? What did he know but the long low glide, the crying out, and the quick and final abyss? I tried to act casual. But I felt like a creature from another age, cowering now beneath his outraged, unshakable vision.

As I came outside again, he sang his lyrical howl across the marsh, and the wild ones answered him.

I walked back to the lounge with their calls in my ears. The light was still on in there.

I entered and looked urgently around me, needing and fearing the sight of the boy. There he was, just picking up the phone, looking smaller than I remembered somehow, his features asymmetrical. He put the phone down when he saw me, because we were the only people in the room, and it was the polite thing to do.

"Hey," he said.

"Hey," I said, trying not to panic at the surprise of our voices, "I was just stopping in . . ."

"That's cool," he said, glancing at me, but with the phone still under his hand. "How are you?"

I wondered if he would think it strange that I was out of breath. "Are you going to make a phone call?"

He hesitated. "I guess in a minute . . ."

The silence swelled then like a great boastful thing, and I felt like I'd never before been alone with anyone until now. There were only two people here. Only one connection that could be made. I realized I had created a situation I didn't know what to do with. I didn't even know him. But I was hurtling forward, like I was still running—running toward him, into him.

"Can I see your yurt sometime?"

He relaxed and gave me his half-grin. "Nope."

"Why?"

"Because. No girls allowed."

I smiled back and, without taking a breath, said, "I want you."

He looked down. He ran the fingertips of his other hand back and forth across the counter.

"What?" he said.

He didn't believe in magic. I would never let him know how hungrily I stood in the cage of the owl, crying with all of my mind, *How shall I approach him?* But he looked so alone and lovely there, his head hanging between his high youthful shoulders, indoors and out of his element, looking down at his hands.

"I want you," I said again, and I felt like laughing.

"But I mean," he said, "do you want me physically? Or . . ." And he lost the rest of his assurance suddenly, and his face fell open and hung still, like a photograph. "Or more than that?"

Then I did laugh, like I didn't care, stalking him from a side angle. "More what?" But of course I knew what he meant. He wanted a girl who could take care of herself, who would never need him. The shame started to fall over me like warm water.

In real life he flirted all the time, with the female researchers and even the young girls. He was like a puppy the women would sigh at and push away, while he begged to be stroked. But now I was offering him something he hadn't asked for. He didn't know what to do with it.

So I wasn't surprised when he sealed his face with a slight, nonspecific smile and said simply, "I have to make a phone call."

I stood there alone and foolish as he carried the receiver into the other room, hearing his loud, guy voice on the phone, and the relief in it.

And I went back outside.

The writer lives in a madness. She is mad. It is impossible to communicate madness to a sane person, who takes sanity for granted, the way you take being alive for granted.

I might return from my mad wanderings and see people hanging about in some indoor place, and they might pause in their laughter and say casually, How was your walk? And it is impossible, as always, to communicate aloneness to company.

I have my writing. That is mine.

It keeps me in my aloneness. But someday, maybe, it will connect me with the world, whatever the world is—without my ever having to speak.

I came to my own cabin and stood looking into it like its emptiness was a whole sentence about loneliness. I knew the invitation I had made to the boy would not go unanswered, because it is not the kind of invitation a boy ignores. But the excitement of fear fell again, like a veil, and gave way to a duller, more familiar sorrow.

A sorrow like cages and flightless wings. A sorrow that was far easier for me than speaking or relating to any other human being.

I couldn't go in yet. It was just beginning to snow now, the white flakes emerging suddenly out of nowhere like a hundred thousand tiny white knights galloping swiftly down the mountain of the darkness.

I stood so still my very breath was for a moment an ecstasy, and I watched as an artist watches—watched the spaces between the flakes as they filled with the substance of imagination.

And I could hear nothing but the actual sound of every single snowflake falling. And each lisp upon the earth sounded utterly important—its sweet sticky sound like a twinkling light, like a single wet star.

The sound of tenderness.

Had he ever heard this? The silence, I mean. This silence deep enough, complete enough, unpretentious enough, that you could actually pray inside it. Not a silence that roars or booms, but a silence like fur and skin. A silence that quiets your mind instantly without you even trying. It does not hum or whir or spook you in any way. It isn't a loud silence, or a padded silence. It does not make you feel tiny or insignificant. It is not grand or impossible to comprehend.

It's just a silence with the sound of your breath inside. A silence in which you feel you have unexpectedly come upon God Itself, whatever God is, and It is sleeping. Yes God, sleeping hot and close to your face, breathing. The body of a god right next to you, pink and breathing, like a baby.

This is what a snowfall sounds like, and someday I would show him this, like he showed me the stories of the animals. The stories I couldn't see without him.

A snowfall sounds like this. Like everything you want is as close as it could possibly be, without ever touching you.

Speech is hardly even possible for me. Speech is hemmed in by the confines of the ordinary living world, and broken by the proximity of another body.

I mean imagine that I said all this aloud to you, in these words, in the ordinary world.

No, of course not. Never.

This is the loneliness. This.

Five

Sometimes I am tossed up on a sudden throne of joy: the sun roars into being as if for the first time, a great foam of light easing from its nest of clouds.

One day the trees made a tickling motion, a motion that just fell out of stillness like water. Because someone was walking toward me, just as I happened to think of him.

I used to believe in signs—omens of the future. But beauty has no time in it, only rhythm. And as your body becomes more accustomed to this rhythm, the things that happen come closer and closer to the things you want to happen.

In the morning after my unanswered invitation, as I began my walk to the shed, I heard him walking behind me. I turned around and saw him, and then I thought that I should wait, because it would be rude not to, though I did not know if he would want to walk with me. I waited. My longing at this time was sweet and light. The not knowing whether he would walk with me—the not knowing, in itself—was like some precious freedom. I blew like a small morning fairy into the grand nothing of possibility.

By the time he was close enough for me to see the shadows of his feet as he lifted them, I could tell by his down-turned eyes that he would. My heart, as if it had been dreaming elsewhere until now, plunged back in. My body remembers this feeling still: a dark becoming, like spilled ink spreading over the page.

I loved his presence beside me, thick and alive, his spirit a coil of snakes just waking and licking the air. He lifted his chin, told me which birds were making their spring calls already, pointed to things that I could not have noticed through the blur of his presence.

Finally he said, "So what kind of crazy stuff were you saying to me last night anyway?"

I said, "I don't know. I had just gone for a walk, a night walk ..." But then I stopped. I wished he could know what that meant—how exquisite my life was when no one was looking.

He came into the shed with me to prepare for his morning reptile presentation. I had not held one of the snakes yet but he lifted one out of its aquarium and handed it to me with both hands, grinning. "Will you hold my snake?"

I reached up with my own hands, laughing, thinking how wild and sexy and lonely both of us were, like no one else. The snake eased up my arm and tasted my neck—his body a weight both slow and shocking, completely without tenderness.

"What did you think? You think I'm crazy, then?" I asked suddenly.

Desire lurked in the corners, in the folds of our clothing, between our numb lips.

He lifted his chin as if trying to be a grown-up, and answered in a distant, swollen voice,

"I think you're interesting."

A doe in the forest, at that certain time of autumn.

The male behind her, struggling. It is much more difficult than even the battle of bone against bone, the meeting of the males head-on in the torn, twilit clearing. More difficult even than the year and the year before, when he had to wait so long, sidling along the peripheries of doe herds, ejaculating against his stomach, too small to be noticed.

Now perhaps he is too large. Every moment of his life has been graceful. But penetration requires him to fling his whole body upward, and then flail, with his head flung back and the massive grace of his flesh uprooted and clawing the nothing like some over-turned insect—all balancing on that single point below.

The point of entry.

She braces herself on the earth, breathing the cold steady dawn, bearing the contortions of the male—his urgency, his falling, his fear.

The aspens around the clearing are so still. The oaks have already begun to empty themselves of leaves. The air is a skeleton, the lush flesh of summer long ago ravaged and gone, and the wind scrapes the open nerves of the forest and the body of the doe as he leaves her now—as she shudders into this oblivious pregnancy.

Imagine this: the stillness, and the doe. The doe remaining in the middle of the cold autumn as if she had always been alone.

And a single leaf falling. A single autumn leaf whose path through the air splits the world arbitrarily in two: summer and winter, male and female . . .

Halfway to the ground it begins to whirl.

~

We saw a deer once, the boy and I. Sometime after the first time he was inside me, but before the second or third time, when he had me, and I lost him.

She stood in the middle of the trail, watching us realize she was there. In the moment before she fled, the boy was silent. And I knew that he was silent for me. He was silent in the way that a boy is silent when he has not yet made his conquest, when he does not yet know his own power. When he still follows the unspoken instructions of the girl—anything to get closer to the body he wants without seeming to want it. No matter how aloofly he turned from me, I could count on this wanting.

Long ago in the days of Celtic lore, deer belonged to the Other World. And often a faerie woman would come to a hunter at the edge of night, disguised as an albino doe. And when he chased her she would move away, and though she did not seem to run, though she seemed in fact to walk at the most even and graceful pace, his hounds could not bound fast enough to catch her. And before he knew it he would find himself lost in a forest he did not seem to know, though he had spent his life in those hills, and surrounded by a fog so thick he could not see his own feet. And all he could hear was music at once so liltingly beautiful and splendidly haunting that he stumbled through the fog entranced, and at the mouth of death fell to his knees with irreversible desire . . .

But what was I but a shy girl, who could not make things into spoken words? The deer hesitated there, the line of her back turned fuzzy in the open light of the trail, not knowing yet whether or not to be afraid.

"Deer are my favorite animal," was all I could say.

But he must have heard the fairy tale in my voice, and the danger in it; the moment broke. His laughter was like pavement over wild fields as he turned to walk away. "Why do you love them so much? They're everywhere. They're a nuisance."

I turned to follow him, incredulous. "It doesn't matter," I said. "To me they're magic."

He looked embarrassed. "There's too many deer. Some of them aren't even native. Hell, we should shoot them." And when I didn't say anything he added, "We have endangered plants growing here, endangered butterflies that feed on those plants, and these stupid overpopulated deer wipe them out."

The passion in his voice undid me. I'd helped with a research project once where they'd captured elk with helicopters to relocate them. I'd watched the nets fall out of the helicopters over their running, and as the nets enclosed them they'd tripped and somersaulted over the ground like fragile figurines. Yet I knew it was the right thing to do. At least I thought I did.

I stood beside him, thinking about beauty and its eerie resemblance to truth.

For example this burning in the throat—and this pressing of the heart against the breast bone like a child with her face pressed against the glass—was this love?

"There must be a reason," I said.

"A reason for *what?*"

"A reason I find deer so beautiful."

"Yeah, because you're a girl. You're weird."

"No, I'm serious."

He laughed. "I'm not serious. Maybe that's your problem."

It's not about you, I wanted to say, my face flushing, but it was.

Later, I kept remembering the reflection of myself in the deer's frightened stare.

It was as if in that moment, when the boy still respected my silence, I was alone with her.

I remembered drinking in the texture of her body, which I could feel in my chest. We do not see only with our eyes, I thought. I had felt her, rough and bony and warm, her face incapable of expression as we know it.

And I remembered how—it was the wind, or my voice—everything had changed.

Her frozen pose had melted, and she had recognized us. I had felt embarrassed suddenly, a tumult of molecules surprised into self-awareness, trying to rearrange itself into an alert being. Everything that I, human, had witnessed in the nature of the deer was stilled by the sight of me: human. She forgot her path through the forest and I forgot my fairy tale thoughts, and we drew a blank together for an instant, between an answerless question and a disconnected answer.

I felt my own body, pulsing like a light.

Would we chase her? She wanted to know. Were we predators? Were we hungry?

When I spoke, her ears strained forward, holding the sound of me taut inside. What was this? In the tilt of her ears, her singular gaze, the slope of her neck so coherent with her poised body, I saw that I was human.

Speaking with my human voice, saying I loved her.

And human, I could not have answered simply. Yes, it was some kind of starving hunger that I felt. Yes, I would chase her forever, but in another way that she could not understand.

Yet in that moment before she ran from me, I felt hurt. How could she look at me so distantly, as if I did not know her? She could look at the boy that way perhaps, but not at me. I had watched deer from hidden places all my life. I had heard the crack of antlers striking together like slow avalanches; I had watched doe and fawn sneak away together into endlessly yellow meadows; I had seen the exhaustion of herds in the snow; I knew them. It was as if my secret crush turned and saw me suddenly, surprised as at a stranger, not knowing that I'd watched her cry so many times before when she thought she was alone.

I could not answer for myself. Yet as she folded her body hastily back into the shadows, and the shadows of the trees ruffled and settled again like the feathers of some great protective bird around her, and I lost her forever to that other world in which she would continue the unseen beauty of living without me, I was somehow relieved.

The boy began to speak, but the deer was far away, safe in my fairy tale.

It is not aloneness that is lonely. The loneliness is somewhere else—somewhere in the encounter with another, when aloneness becomes no longer enough.

And the only time I would taste the exact same flavor of loneliness again would be when the boy, having collapsed in sleep against my breasts, then rose and peeled himself from me, and worst of all, looked back at me with the fears of a human being all over his faraway face, as if he did not recognize the animal inside me that loved him.

I learned to hold a raptor on my fist.

I would go into the cage, looking away like I was going somewhere else, like I was not even there. I lifted my arm, with the leash wrapped around it, to the hawk's perch. I looked away so that neither of us would have to bear the fear that my face caused her. I tried to make my mind a smooth globe in which her presence was perfectly contained, for I began to sense the power of my thoughts, and to realize that if my mind broke away for even a moment—to fantasize that she could love me, for example, or to fantasize that the boy would be impressed by her love for me—she would fly away. And if she flew across the cage and I had to try again, then I had failed.

I felt the fragile interplay of my thoughts and her presence, until I wondered if the strength of my focus alone could hold her still.

I tried to talk to her with my mind. But I didn't really believe in what I was doing. I did not really believe in exposing her to that hot room before the great crowd of people, for I knew I would not be willing to do that even to myself. And yet I held out my fist to her and insisted on it—insisted that she come with me to the carrying case, and then to the boy, who would present her to the humans.

I had to hold out my fist like it was anything to offer. Like she could ever respond with those hard golden feet out of any impulse other than fear—fear bound and woven into all of her muscles, quiet and essential to life itself, as she obediently stepped up.

No matter what I did, those frightened eyes never moved from my face. I tried to be gentle. I tried to be a tree. Sometimes I tried to love her, and sometimes I tried to be nothing. But it did not matter. I remained only the offering of the fist, the force that forced her feet to lift, one by one, and grasp—lightly, but with potential for harm.

During the raptor presentations the boy stood in the hot room before the crowd, with winter floating voiceless and melancholy at the windows, and the children gasped that he could hold an eagle on his fist.

I gasped too, without showing it, for I loved the easy strength, the careless calm, with which he stood and waited while the eagle pounded the remains of his wings against the dull air, flailed off and swung upside down, grasped the boy's patient fist in a terror, and finally drew himself upright again with a dramatic reshuffling of black and white feathers.

The eagle was the only one I was not strong enough or brave enough to hold. But I knew that eagle. I fed him every day. I knew the cage he stalked, littered with the delicate rainbow of fish scales. I watched him in my spare time, wondering if there was anything in a human being he could recognize. One of his wings had been amputated in his youth, after he fell from a tree in a storm, his car-sized nest shredded in the wind behind him as he landed on the mundane earth where he should have died.

I don't know what he did all day: he could not fly at all. He moved little, for by nature well-fed raptors rarely need to. I wondered, if there is nothing to hunt and nothing to fear, what does one do in the stillness?

Often when left alone—or even while we stood there, as if he were distracted from us by some real thought in his mind— he spent long moments staring down at his perched feet. No one could explain this. Even now he was doing it, as the boy stood there talking about him to the crowd of children.

Maybe, I thought, in my own long moments of distraction, he was staring past his feet, beyond to nothing. Maybe this bird who was born to spend his life looking down from cliff-tops, who had lost his whole life before he ever experienced it, was looking—without knowing it—for the sky.

"So we're going out on the town later—are you girls coming?"

He said it with a half-grin, and with all the necessary irony of knowing the town was nothing but one bar, one store, two restaurants and one post office, ten miles away.

Would he have invited me were it not for this other girl who stood beside him now, this girl I had never seen before? They had been standing there talking, and I had paused as I passed them, riveted painfully by the light of his smile—which he turned from her to me like a sort of after-thought.

"Hey," he'd called out to me graciously from within the ring of their closeness.

And now that I stood with them he looked to us as one entity: blurred-together pieces of a miracle called "girl" that he wanted to get close to. I wondered again if he would have asked me, just me, if she hadn't been there. I wondered if I would have decided to go, had he not asked me himself.

I spent that night mostly alone, at the bar with a drink I didn't drink, wanting not to be seen and yet feeling torn apart by the judgment I imagined in their not seeing me. It wasn't that I wanted to be lonely, I thought. I could almost love these young homeless people of wilderness, at least more than anyone else I would ever love. But it was so difficult to go that distance, because they could never understand the wanting in my love—how in reality I wanted more than them: I wanted to die and become animal, and be inside them, and not have to try to talk anymore.

But we could only talk. We could only communicate in that age-old speaking language, the only language we knew we knew.

They would never know how for me there was a singing embedded in the winter silence, and how the wind could always tell me what I was thinking.

Because maybe each one of us was our own home, each

miles away from the other, with a common language but no common earth. Like in one of those really inefficient suburban projects where I grew up, with houses spread out so far that no one ever sees each other except through car windows and dreams, so far apart that all the wild places we could have held in common were cut into little pieces and destroyed.

And I was the only one who carried the loneliness. Even later, only I would carry the loneliness of remembering.

To my left sat the man I'd met on the first day, with the raccoon hands, and the hunched, raccoon shoulders. I didn't mind him sitting there. He was telling me about his studies on the predation of some ground-nesting water bird whose name I do not remember, because I did not recognize it. It was not a bird I had come to know personally, in my lonely hours, and so its name meant nothing to me. But as I listened, I thought of the love that must inspire him to study this bird—a love that he would never speak.

The raccoon man was like the dry soles of your feet in a walk across the desert. He was like the hum of the sea in the bodies of snails, or a long, sadly-smiling sigh. I felt safe with him, and did not want him.

As he spoke I watched the boy. Indeed a thing becomes more romantic, more thrilling, if you focus on it as if it were the only thing. I watched his fire, and the way his body loved itself when he walked, jolting cockily upwards with every step. I watched the way his jeans hung off his ass, and the hook of his black grin under the sharper hook of his raptor nose as he flirted and made his rounds, the cold wild still fizzing off his body. I had to keep track of him because he could not be still, and I knew that as soon as he left, all the color would drain from the room. In fact I did not really have to watch. If he was near me I could feel his presence in the vividness of my own body.

"He's such a shmoozer, isn't he," the raccoon man said,

watching him with me for a moment. The boy was flirting with that other girl, whoever she was. The long swells of her hair had the serenity of snow. The indent of her back had the same slant as the oak trees that grew tilted over the lake and never fell. She moved, I thought, like one of the lynxes that had been hunted to extinction in this forest long ago. And I imagined she held some mystery that the boy lusted after.

But later he came to sit on the other side of me.

"Are you enjoying your deep thoughts?" he said.

I looked at him.

"Stop flirting with me," he said.

"I'm not!"

"Yes you are. You're so easy to read. Did you know that?"

No . . . and what did he know? Did he know me, suddenly?

"We're not sleeping together, okay? We work together," he said, his grin simmering up from his down-turned face.

"No we don't. Not really."

"That's true," he answered, with the confident inconsistency of a drunk, looking up from his lap, and then off toward a different pretty girl.

What happened that day in the valley of foxes, when that story I thought I knew was interrupted by the scribble of his sudden passage?

Why did all the words I wrote after that sound foolish, like fingers grasping at flight?

And why did I want this boy? This boy who was indeed nothing but a boy, simple and eager, not even a man. It is the mystery itself that fascinates me. Even now I wake to him in my dreams, as he strides arrogantly from one end of my memory to the other, with his icy grace.

Or maybe it is nothing but the ache of my own self that haunts me, the ache of my own hiding soul.

For in fact that was the winter I became real.

That night as I lay in my bed with the darkness piling in, knowing he would come to my cabin—*knowing* he would—I felt afraid. It was an instinctual fear, as if someone were coming to kill me.

I feared the image I imagined of his face in my doorway, when he would suddenly appear, ready to fulfill the flirtation, ready to give me exactly what I had asked for.

But I never saw him. He did not need a light. I heard the delicious secrecy of the door sliding open, and in the next moment the darkness took form and became his weight on the bed and his mouth on my neck—kisses with the urgent confidence of assured possession.

"Are you drunk?" I asked.

"Only a little," he said, uninterested in the question.

It was his face I most ached to curve my hands to. The rest of the body is like a wave once touched—as easy, almost, as sleep. But the face purses preciously with those poignant inhibitions. It seemed wild and forbidden somehow, to touch his face with my crude hands: that shape of visual, mental expression now released in ecstasy. How I longed to find in the dark the sly aggressive corner of his chin, the tender trunk of his neck, and its muscles arching for the kiss. And the full, unhesitating depth of his mouth, and the scrappy tumble of his hair all over my fingers.

He didn't know, as he tried out all his own fantasies, violent and contorted, how I loved to touch his face. How it turned in my palm heedlessly, and thus with heedless gentleness, vaguely wondering at my touch but lost in the eagerness of the body's whims.

When we finally lay still I could hear the willowy howl of coyotes across the lake: first an eerie whistling, and then their yipping like a flashing of gold coins in the darkness, and finally their full-fledged demonic laughter. I loved that he could hear this with me. I lay breathing, imagining the depth of the cold just outside my window, and us out of its reach.

I was falling, level by level, like a leaf slipping side to side and ever downward through the levels of the wind, into the depth of him. I was unraveling into soil, melting into water, dissolving into elements, unthinking.

"You know, I need to get out of this place." His words were level and gentle, just barely above the sound of my silence. I didn't open my eyes.

"Why?"

"I don't know. I hate teaching. I want to be out on my own."

"But you're good at teaching. You're making a difference. Everybody loves you."

"No they don't. They don't even know me."

"What do you mean?" My eyes were open now. I lifted my chin just slightly from his chest and looked up toward his face. I could feel the space between my heart and his.

"Nothing. Whatever."

"Maybe you don't let them know you."

"Yeah. That's true."

But it didn't seem like a revelation. It seemed like a conversation he was having with himself, perhaps not even connected with me.

"I should go back to my cabin soon," he said.

"Why?"

"Because. That's where I sleep."

There was a smaller, tighter silence then, as I tried to listen to the coyotes again, but could not hear them. I saw myself broken and scattered, little shards of useless humanity.

"Don't think I'm coming in here every night," he added. "Okay?"

His skin seemed suddenly ugly against my own. I sat up in the bed, like I could go somewhere, like I could be the one to escape. Escape him, escape me, escape the cold disparity between us and not us.

"Just go away now then," I said.

He laughed. "Why?"

"Because you're making me sad," I said helplessly, frustrated by how simple such a word sounded. "Just don't stay at all."

"Shhh." He took my hand dutifully and brought it around to his smooth boy chest, and I lay down behind him because I had to. The humble heat of his body in contrast to the cold words felt so terribly good. He had the fibrous muscles of a hunter.

My own softness scared me.

He fell asleep for an hour, before he woke and left me. And in that time, in which I did not sleep, the pain I felt was like a light in the darkness. Like a light I could see myself by, that told me, as if for the first time, that I was alive.

I wasn't going to die after all.

SPRING

Who are you, then, Glorious Singer?
Midnight sleeps, in harmony with
deep forest oblivion.
You startle yourself, gnaw yourself.
Yet who are you? The vast river surges
beyond the horizon.

-Yang Mu

Bats folded like dark handkerchiefs in the eaves. Buried in a sleep deeper than sleep, deeper than life itself. Folded like little deaths in the recesses of winter.

And the raccoon asleep too in his den, his cunning and his eager human hands asleep, and also the skunk asleep inside his tail—with the stripes along his spine like a long yin-yang tracing the pathway of his life. And the badger, in a system of rooms he built himself, under the stiff, now frozen earth, also sleeping.

The weasel dashes up and down and between the trees like a deadly little flame, never still. He darts like a white tooth to the throat of the rabbit; he is the only one who will be able to find the vulnerable belly of the porcupine, who is gripping the tree branches with his muscular tail and grunting his warning in the tree-lined dawn.

The owl is listening in the sky. She can hear the raccoon stirring restlessly in his sleep. She can hear the squirrel drinking from the thin slit of liquid between the ice and the shore. She can hear the heartbeats of the meadow voles as they tremble beneath the snow, unable to still the signs of their helpless aliveness, no matter how quiet they keep. She can hear the huge steps of the girl who is always lost, who echoes without meaning to.

The owl can hear these things all the way from the sky.

And the owl hears the call of the coyote, who calls as if he doesn't care who hears him. He can hunt with others or alone. He can plot hunting strategies with the badger, and he has fucked wolves and dogs alike. He can live anywhere, and he will eat anything he can kill.

The coyote is aware of the doe as she becomes weaker and easier to hunt, and of the fawn in her belly who will be even easier. A season ago when the leaves were falling, he listened as the stag betrayed himself with mournful bellowing—the stag who in his longing for the doe was for once oblivious to danger. The coyote—wasn't it him, lithe and ghostly?—was creeping close to the heat of those bodies as they lost themselves together. He circled around them hungrily, his senses shining through the trees, for in the helplessness of their union—in the very moment of their fulfillment, with their bodies twisted in the most vulnerable of positions—he could taste their death.

The winter continues now as if spring were impossible. The doe is used to starving and surviving, but so is the coyote.

He knows all of her pathways. He knows her last hold-outs, the spaces around the bodies of the oldest trees where the snow is thinner and she can still find a mouthful of nourishment. He knows the stands of young aspens she has already stripped bare, and the stands she will move to tomorrow morning. He knows every stage of her weakness, and the tremor in her fleshless legs as she lowers her pregnant belly to the ground in the deep of night. He knows how far she can run.

And she knows that he knows. She has known him since the beginning of time. She knows that terror of being alive: she felt it when she was born, and when the stag thrust his life inside her. She can feel the impossible heat of her own blood in the cold.

She can feel the coyote's hunger in her own body, like empathy.

Six

I knew nothing of killing.

I knew nothing about the opening of the body in the night, the need, the certainty and rightness and who knows what kind of mercy in the grasp of the raptor's talons—that ancient embrace, in which death and life fold seamlessly together.

I wouldn't admit to the boy that I was afraid to start killing the rats myself. How could I be afraid of a small bin with a blanket over it, and a gas tank with the hose inserted inside it like a thin ugly penis? It was such an easy, harmless way to die. Nothing gruesome.

Maybe that was what scared me—the understatement of it. Gentle as a dream, but when you wake you find out it was real.

I had never killed an animal. I didn't eat meat. I didn't even kill mosquitoes.

The first day I had to do it, I stood in front of the rat cages for a long time, and listened to the untimed, unromantic shufflings inside. And I thought about the raptors' hunger.

I knew about hunger. I knew about desire.

But that wasn't enough—that knowledge. It seemed there was something more to killing than hunger. Another step I hadn't learned yet.

Maybe that's why the stories still wouldn't come.

One day I went into the raptor cages singing.

I heard my own voice very faintly. Not my speaking voice, which scared me, but this other, small song voice. A voice like a child with flushed skin, who, beneath the cover of her silence, wanted it all—wanted to run out to the middle of the lake in the middle of the night even though people can't stand on water.

I sang softly to the raptors, hoping they would know by my singing that I, too, did not believe in cement or cages or harsh voices.

I sang to myself, and to the little bodies of the rats that I lay on the perches, as if singing them to sleep, feeding them to the angels. And the angels clacked their beaks but did not fly away yet: they let me come closer.

But far off in the silence, I heard the black snake hiss, and then immediately the boy was there. And not only that, but the raccoon man with him.

"What are you doing?" the boy asked. His presence there needed no explanation. He was coming to cage the raptors and bring them out for the evening presentations.

"Nothing," I said, horrified, and ashamed of my shame. The Great-horned Owl flew away. Maybe it wasn't my singing that had kept him still after all, but the way my singing had distracted *me*—for one moment—from my own humanness.

"Do they appreciate your singing?" asked the raccoon man,

smiling. Then he turned to the boy and teased him. "Look—maybe that old owl likes her. He always flies away when you come in."

The boy raised his eyebrows carelessly, looking at me as if I were the one who'd challenged him. "It's an owl. Animals don't like or dislike. We're predator or prey to them, that's all."

Then he turned and said to the raccoon man, "Okay, time to conquer the eagle."

And it was as if I poured the poem of my spirit out of my flesh then and hid it behind me, as I waited for them to leave. It might have looked as if I stood there and felt nothing.

But when their voices were distant enough I poured my spirit back into me, and felt my face blur, and began murmuring to the owl—as he huddled fearfully in his corner—about emotions he could not recognize. Why couldn't I explain myself?

There are no words for innocence. It is a greater rebellion in this world than any kind of vulgarity.

"What did you do to that girl?" I heard the raccoon man say lightly. "She can hardly speak when she's around you."

And the boy's reply was worse, because I could not hear it.

I wished I could tell him what I was.

I wished I could tell him with what delicacy came the spattering of wind and light sometimes, through the meadow groves of fir.

How the air lilted in under the needles, like prayer, the needles rippling together like one soft substance that I could feel all over me as I watched them, like cream.

How the boughs shuffled together without ever quite touching or making a sound. Not swaying with any particular direction, but only emerging, swiftly and with grace.

The movement occupied the stillness—was a shade, a shift of stillness. As if my vision perceived another vision; as if the wind passed a window of motion before the image of the trees that only I could see.

Say you had a child. And you watched her sleep. And her breath was so contented that you could barely perceive the motion of it at all, but for the very slight lifting and falling of a single lock of hair grazing the pillow near her lips. How you would feel as you watched that lock tremble in her breath (the smallest of movements, and yet brimming with the bloom of your child's whole life)—that is how the mere and silent shuffle of the fir trees moved me. Every time I ever saw it, I became weightless inside myself, and I was plunged into a giant satisfaction of love, weak with gratitude to know that so much could be given with no effort at all.

I spent days walking along the deer paths, listening with my whole body.

I took my desire for the boy—the dream of it, the tangled, contradictory question of it—and lay it down upon the line of the wind in the trees, like a ribbon. I watched to see if it was comfortable in the pattern there, for to me this pattern was truth. And I watched the face of the wind for an answer.

I followed the deer. I followed the traces of the deer, their footprints flooding the forest, and I walked with their extreme gentleness. I saw the muddled torrent of their paths in the snow, and I knelt where they had lain in the tussled shelter of the firs. I gathered the quill-shaped hairs. I lay my cold-hardened fingers against the bowl of their rest, and then I lay my body there, and tried to understand the warmth of frozen ground.

Your longing will stretch your soul wider, said the wind bursting spaces into the trees.

Pay attention to the animals, said the grouse who exploded from the thicket—who was right beside me all along without my noticing.

I remember some moments and not others. I remember most the moments when I saw myself from outside, in someone else's eyes. Or the moments when I felt him inside my body.

Like the day I experienced his expression in my own face, and thus glimpsed his spirit—that inner world that made him as uncomfortable as the outer human world made me.

It was about a bird. The bird leapt off a tree branch and fell through the air, then flapped and rose, then paused and fell again, then flapped and rose, and continued away like that in little loops: giving in and rising.

"What kind of bird flies like that?" he tested me.

"It's a woodpecker," I said.

"Good!" he said, and his patronizing incredulity annoyed me, but I found myself turning away and smiling anyway, pleased with his praise in spite of myself. And in the downward motion of my eyes and the line of my closed, smiling lips—in the tension of my jaw at that moment, and the simultaneous wriggle of my heart—I recognized him somehow. I thought of his subtle, secret grin as he looked down at his hands the night I asked him to sleep with me. Somehow this was the smile I knew I felt in my own face. And I knew suddenly that he wanted to be liked as much as I did, in spite of his distance, in spite of his insistence that he would never spend a night with me.

I looked at him and laughed.

"What?" he asked, and I felt his curiosity hungering at the edges of his confidence. He kept staring straight ahead.

"Oh nothing," I said. "It's just... I felt like you for a second."

"What do you mean?" He was suspicious now. I imagined

him standing lost and afraid inside himself, glancing swiftly about, seeing ghosts.

I felt bolder now. "I realized you actually like me."

For a moment I thought I had him. There was a space where none of the usual responses were possible, where he just stood there—himself.

Then he rolled his eyes.

"Of course I like you," he said impatiently, sighing as if looking down at the pointless musings of a child. "Why wouldn't I like you?"

Then he lurched away again, shaking off the stillness—hunting.

What did he seek in his lone forays? And how did he find all the things that I missed, the things he boasted about in the evening when they sat around in the lounge—like the remains of a yearling deer who didn't last the winter, or the clawing of wings in the bloody snow where some heavenly thing came down and broke the skull of a rodent?

Perhaps it was because he did not think. Because he did not stop to wonder, or to imagine, far away in his mind, what it would really be like to live like the mice in that strange purgatory of nothingness between earth and snow.

I had asked to go with him today—asked him to teach me again what he knew. But it wasn't as I'd imagined, because maybe what I had asked was not really what I wanted.

He led me across the lake. He stayed just ahead of me. I ached to know what the silence of this ever-speaking, ever-moving, unceasing boy of the world was made of. Now suddenly he was closed, private—like he got sometimes. He stopped. In the middle of the lake—just stopped there, for no reason.

His back was to me. I wondered suddenly about his mother, his father, what questions he'd asked when he was a little boy.

He was looking out at the lake—not at an animal, or a track or a sign, or anything in particular that I could see, but almost as if, for a moment, he saw the nothing that haunted me.

I stopped too, and felt the wind sweep by, wrapping me in its infinity so that I almost felt okay. I had stood like this on days and nights alone, and listened to the lake boom softly. I had stood way out here on the ice, when the sky too was ice, and the wind was cold, and all around me was nothing—nothing pressing into all distances beyond me. And the grand openness of that nothing had protected me from anyone who could ever see me, or critique me, or break me down into some human form I could not rest comfortably inside. The silence was so big, bigger than all my mind and my questioning.

But I could not rest easy in the big space of my aloneness today. All my being flooded into the unknown silence of the boy. I hardly knew where I was.

The wind died and the boy turned around, and recognized me again. Our eyes met and we didn't say anything, but his face had softened in some strange way that felt good. He smiled. Just a little twitch of a smile, and it did not reach his eyes though his eyes were glowing with something else—and I thought that we shared some understanding.

In that little moment of a smile I saw the possibility of all the sorrow and helplessness and suffering love that humanness is named for. All that would never be said.

"Are you cold?" he asked half-absently, heedless of the shock of such gentleness.

"I'm fine," I answered too fast, but moved imperceptibly toward him.

"Come on, I'll show you something," he said, and was off again.

At the edge of the lake, the long grasses hissed in the wind like the swipe of a thigh against the sheets at night. He knelt to show me the rows of rectangular tooth marks in a fallen aspen.

"Do you know what made those?"

Beaver. Out in the frozen water, I saw the hump of their lodge, an unremarkable island of carefully placed sticks that looked completely haphazard.

I imagined the generations of beavers inside that lodge, discussing whether or not their food cache would last the winter, dimly haunted by instinctual memories of wolves that stalked the edges of their watery haven.

And I imagined the inside of the boy's mind, hidden and silent and afraid of something he had no words for.

"What do you think about when you're alone out here?" I asked, trying to be casual.

"Why?"

"I just want to know."

"I don't know. Whatever's on my mind I guess. Whatever's happening. I don't know. Hey, why do you have to be so fucking deep? Can't you just be here?"

Fear rose up in hot fountains from my belly, burning my heart. I had not seen it coming at all. But maybe he had seen my questions coming from a long way off, before I even knew I would ask them. I retreated quickly into my silence, and frantically traced the tooth marks with my fingers, looking away.

He said, "Okay, look, maybe I like it because I can just be myself here. When people are around they're always wanting things from me, trying to change me, pressuring me. You know?"

I did. I thought of standing in the center of the lake and dissolving in the silence, forgiven for all my desire, my suffering, my humanness.

But I said, "Do you think I'm pressuring you?"

"Oh forget it." He shook his head. "You're so serious. Did you come out here to learn to track animals or to analyze my psyche?" He might have been grinning his jester's grin now—I could almost feel it—but I couldn't look.

I didn't want to go. He was already going. He was already walking away. I couldn't move. I wanted to say I was sorry. I wanted to go back to the center of the lake and start over. I couldn't move.

But he could. He was always moving. I couldn't believe he didn't stop when he realized I wasn't following. He just disappeared like wildlife into the darkening forest, and every fading crunch of his footsteps in the snow left a bigger space for my own lonely breath until that was the only thing left.

And I knew, in a way, that he didn't care. He wasn't angry with me, because he didn't really care about me, one way or the other. I wanted to climb out of my body. I wanted to climb up into the trees and follow the dazzling little pattern of their golden twigs up into the shrinking sun and disappear.

But I had to walk now because the smallest parts of my body had become numb. I hurried along the lake's edge, my feet closing in the fragile layer of nothingness beneath the snow where the mice were hiding. I felt that jittery fear of the night, like something was always behind me, whichever way I turned, except that it was light out still, and the night was inside me.

The paths we had traveled seemed like strangers to me now. I didn't care about them; I cared only for the whirlpools in my heart—all liquid and storm. It took me a while to grow conscious of the familiar sick feeling I hadn't felt since my last job, in some other wilderness far away.

I was lost.

But I didn't feel scared this time. I felt angry.

Why? Why hadn't I just followed the water back to a trail I recognized, instead of tramping desperately after his footprints, trying to follow a trail he would never reveal to anyone? It should have been easy enough to follow his footprints, only they didn't go toward home now; they veered off somewhere and went their own way, and now I couldn't remember where we'd started.

I had to follow my own footprints all the way back to the spot where he'd abandoned me, now sizzling cold in the late afternoon light, and then follow the trail we'd made together all the way back, because I hadn't been paying any attention to where we were going when he was leading. I hated the small wavering path of my own unconscious footprints at the edge of his path of certainty.

When I finally arrived at my cabin, I went immediately inside and lay down on my bed. The familiarity of my room seemed meaningless to me. I didn't know what to do. I imagined the boy, and wondered when I would see him again. I knew he wouldn't return until much later, and his lone wanderings made me ache with a restlessness like envy that seemed difficult to bear.

I listened to the owls waking in the forest, and thought about the simple, torturous wonder of another human being's existence in the same universe as mine.

There was a period in the dead of winter when I wasn't writing at all. I just sat in my cabin where the boy had slept long ago, and was fascinated by ideas, and unable to catch them. The animals made ineffable patterns in the night beyond me, and did not know me. I no longer felt real. I felt I was floating just above even my own life.

It's like this. Indoors on a winter day, something happens with the light, and once you've seen it, nothing else seems really important.

You have seen this if you've ever lived in the snowy fields of winter, and then spent here and there a long lonely afternoon indoors when the cold finally kept you there—with a pen in your hand.

I guess at some point the trees must turn to water, and the sun thins to a sheen like waving hair.

Then the light falls where you least expect it—over the papers strewn unaesthetically on the table, or in a corner of the wall behind the bed where no one ever looks—and startles you out of contemplation, out of all the passion of your inward moment. It flickers with a restless, tireless grace, shimmering into shadow and returning again.

It is just the reflection of the light through the pine needles, you understand—but somehow within the nodding, shifting, and balancing of that pale light you seem to see at once such intimacy and such melding of motion, it seems the very soul of life is shivering inside itself there, whatever that could mean.

There is not one shape you could hold onto.

They stutter, these fringes of light, poignant and riveting like the last broken scenes projected from an old, black and white, family film projector. You are suddenly aware of a silence all over you, a winter silence underlying all things, present even during conversation and music and all the other noises of the day.

Like a sound so faithful you've gotten used to it, and forgotten it was there—this silence. The light whistles with silence—with the needles blowing in the winter wind—and is never still, and never rowdy.

When I came upon that light during a day alone in the cabin, I was overcome by the vividness of my heart, and I thought this is it—this is everything. And yet, what was it? Just light, just silence. Something you could never bring yourself to think of when it is gone.

I could write a whole story about nothing but that light—the layers of it, how they fall over each other, dream upon dream, rhythmless and fragile and wild. That silence we were born with, that rhymes with everything.

But it is not enough.

In those long-ago days of story, when enchantment came in the form of an albino deer, people could not bear the winter.

They dreamed of an Other World, where everything was opposite. While winter turned their bones brittle and their hearts dim, and stole their children and hid the animals from them, they dreamed that in the Other World was eternal summer, eternal life.

It was the doe, at times in the form of a beautiful woman, who led the hunters with that music of pure imagination—a music that made them forget their cold and hunger—into what was, in the end, both their paradise and their doom.

But it was in the hot body of the hunt itself, where human turned animal and back again, that a person began to actually shift between worlds.

I couldn't ever climb out of my body.

And I couldn't ever climb out of my life, for the living was lain down in connections that could not be undone.

Like killing.

Every day, or sometimes every other day, I had to kill something.

I guess in the end I just started doing it anyway, without understanding, because I couldn't stand there all day, trying to understand it. Sometimes you have to act before you think.

I picked out the rats with intention.

The littler softer ones (for the screech owl, the kestrel, the snakes) I lifted by their tails, and let them curl around my hands. They clasped the grooves of my knuckles with fingers like tiny starfish, and my hands snuggled into their gently shaking bodies. The eager muscles of their shoulders fit under two fingertips; their noses tapped the small fold of skin between my thumb and forefinger. I placed them lightly in the gassing bin, letting them amble off my palm, jittery and nearsighted.

Maybe I could forgive myself by imagining that I bowed to a more blessed relationship—something bigger than me, that it was not my place to understand: the ancient relationship between the raptor and the rat. Maybe, in these rooms and cages of permanent stillness, it was up to me to keep that story alive, even if I didn't understand it, even if I couldn't yet write it down.

I twisted the gas knob and heard the hiss, and listened to them stop scampering the way the popping of popcorn gradually slows until it is cooked.

I pulled the blanket off the bin and looked in. I was the end of something's life.

I caused that change, that ending.

The body that chose to turn this way, chose to run that way, and sniffed my fingernails curiously, and whose heart beat faster to help it escape and to keep all its organs interacting in that unique rhythm that would never come again—that same body, in the next moment, was still. Because of the motions of my easy hands.

I saw that everything I did had consequence.

After they had lain still for a long time, I leaned close, holding my breath, to see if they were still breathing. When I saw that their stomachs were still, I took one out and laid it on its back in the palm of my hand. I stared at it for several seconds, terrified, waiting for it to twitch. When it did not, I gently pressed its belly with my thumb. Then I pressed its throat in the same way, and then I squeezed its whole body until the organs pressed against the skin with that eerie looseness.

When I felt no pulse still, I finally laid the body aside (its starfish hands slowly easing back down the way grass eases back into place after you step on it), and repeated this procedure on every other body.

Then, to be absolutely sure, I chopped off all their heads before I pressed the knife to their bellies.

Something else—not I, not my dream, a real creature—was dead.

Because of me, living.

How could this be?

My mind could not answer to this. Killing is a paradox. Instead the feeling just grew into me, seeming to enrich my flesh, until the killing, every day, contained a tenderness I had never known before.

Each motion felt full and bright, without thought, as if risen from my gut.

It was I who killed them.

It was I who cut them into pieces.

It was I who laid them on the raptors' perches with a prayer of surrender on my lips.

Imagine you become the wings of the raptors, I told the rats.

Imagine you become the passionate living of the ever-moving rats, I told the raptors with their broken wings and huge, useless eyes.

It was so painful, like being born—the way, after giving the rats this sleep, this eternal dream I longed for, I had to wake to myself and walk out into winter's cold light unmitigated by windows, with a feeling of slow, thick, and inescapable aliveness.

Like their deaths were a part of my hands now. Like loneliness was nothing more than a word. Like what mattered, really, was that I could never again ask my body to perform any gesture which was unimportant.

Seven

Winter became spring through a process of water.

The starkness melted—all the stubborn drama of winter blurred by water, and sloughed off the canvas of the forest in a deluge of tears.

To me the rains of spring were feminine rains. I don't know what gave me the right to believe this. Just the giving in and falling, I guess, of all that water singing and moving over the earth, after all that silence—it felt like forgiveness, like rescue, like a mother.

Rain seemed to want nothing more than to awaken me to my flesh: to unearth me, to press my hair seamlessly against my skin, to soak my skin with the weight of its touch, and to prick me again and again with the thorns of its drops so that I would not forget any part of my body.

That spring I wandered in seas of white lilies that filled the forest without shame. I was able to walk barefoot now, and

I discovered that the soles of my feet knew a language I had never learned. The thawing earth imprinted upon them the stories of fragile running things—their many lives and their decay back into elements—so that my feet learned the whole history of the world and the meaning of both life and death, while my mind swayed dumbly and languorously in the innocence of flowers.

Through my feet I conversed with my shadow: a dark lithe girl who I imagined was utterly carefree, content in her wildness and safe in the earth. I would ask her where to go and she would lead me to the valley of foxes that opened now like a green gift in the heart of the forest.

And I would lie down in the new grasses there and listen to them sigh like the grasses at the beaver pond that the boy loved, and my shadow, pressed invisibly against me now, seemed to tell me that something wonderful would happen here.

The boy was often away now, leading backpacking trips for adolescents. But my longing thrived in the space he left behind.

I carried my longing with me everywhere. It inhabited my world so utterly that it no longer seemed like something so humble as desire, for something so simple as another human being.

These days I lay longing down like petals before me, and I left a wake of longing behind me, so thick I could have used it to find my way home.

There was longing on my breath when I whispered to the raptors, and I lay down to sleep at night with handfuls of longing in my fists. Longing bled from my fingertips when I held the pen above the page, blurring my words before I could get them down.

Some days longing was a song I sang to comfort myself, and some days it was a dead weight I dragged behind me, limping. Some days it was my reason for being, and other days I knew it was merely a pretty gown I wore to smooth my edges and shroud myself against the loneliness.

Sometimes my longing felt as gentle as some pastel bird enfolded in the fuzz of a sunset, or a prism in the frame of a window. And sometimes I would wake alone to longing lying on top of me, like a rough and sluggish beast.

But inside that longing, everything was always beautiful. Long after these days were over, the scent of lilies and wet earth together, or a certain nudging of one shadow against another in a forest of pines, or the wind swooping sensually like a cupped hand over flushed treetops, or the grey body of a lake swelling up inside a loon call would remind me exclusively of the boy.

Not the boy exactly, but my longing for him. For I was completely at home there. Only with the boy next to me, I realized, had desire ever become unbearable.

I kept to myself, save for occasional evening talks with the raccoon man. He sat outside his cabin every evening, always doing something with his hands. Sometimes he was whittling and sometimes he was fixing something, and sometimes he was cooking on a little camp stove. He always called to me as I passed by, and to my surprise I found that sometimes I was okay sitting down on the bench there and letting him talk at me for a while. He didn't seem to mind if I said little in return, but I didn't feel forgotten either. In fact I felt appreciated in some strange, unchallenging way. I did not think he really knew me, and this contented me. I enjoyed his not knowing what I thought about as I watched the rain pour sweetly through the veins of the night.

I thought about the boy.

I wondered if the young girls on his trips had crushes on him.

I thought about the Great Horned Owl, who had begun to hurl himself against his cage at night when the wild ones called, because it was mating season.

The cabin I lived in was crawling with ants. They chose the indentations, the insides of things, the cracks and slits. They ran like a finger up and down the meeting of walls. Like shivers, like unbidden hungers running up and down the insides of my mind, like an itch under my skin. They ran in networks, sticky parades, torrents of tiny motion in some grander rush they created without understanding.

I lay awake and thought I could feel all the animals creeping and trembling around me. The ants uniting in rivers toward sweetness, and the mice whispering in the drawers, and the woodchuck who lived under the cabin crouching fearfully on his pale round haunches. The bats under the roof, waking and flaring up into an eager windy blackness. The moths tossing in the white veils they had woven against the walls. The termites and the beetles eating the very structure of the building that had kept me warm all winter, as if they could never, ever be filled.

There were times, separated from the forest and alone in my room, when longing was a sweaty ghost who lurked in the corner and taunted me. A fickle, transparent ghost—a fairy-devil, with no backside. I fought it then. I told it I did not need it.

But it didn't believe me.

It reminded me again of the problem of the body. My hand upon my belly, brushing the curved hairs. The room was dark and warm, and I couldn't help but remember (it seemed long ago) the boy slipping in after I'd already taken off my clothes, and devouring me.

Longing was the whine of a single mosquito in my ear in the darkness, ceaseless and impossible to source.

One day I lay in the valley of foxes, under the bristling red sumac, because my shadow had brought me there. The sun was high and lovely, and the spring was new enough that warmth was still delicious and unpredictable. It felt like tantalizing feathers on my breasts. It sidled up my neck with the wind. Something about my aloneness in that wild open space consumed me with sexiness.

But it wasn't a sexiness that needed anything. I was sexy the way sunlight was sexy, and what would satisfy sunlight? To be touched by another human being would have seemed harsh and crude.

So when I heard his voice I sat upright fast, as if waking.

"How did you know I was here?" I said, and remembered the tracks in the snow long ago, and remembered the way my shadow had led me here like destiny.

He shrugged. "You're right by a trail."

But I saw in his easy walk toward me, and the way his eyes grazed along the ground and stopped just short of my body, that the moment was not entirely lost on him. He stayed standing.

"Meadows make me feel sexy," I said boldly.

Something seemed to melt in him then, as he grinned and sat down. "Really," he said.

"Something about the openness . . ." I began, and then I remembered the differences between us.

But he was listening, and he looked at me and laughed.

"That's funny," he said, "because I always get horny in forests with big tall erect trees."

I laughed too. "Yeah, well. Maybe that's true. Maybe we turn ourselves on. You know, in land that reminds us of our bodies."

Had I said that?

He didn't seem surprised. He lay back now with his hands folded behind his head. "I always turn myself on. I'm the sexiest person I know."

Laughter. Was it the sunlight? Some strange combination of natural factors? I felt bright and alive in myself, not reaching or longing, content in myself beside him. I was full of wonder, like I'd just come to the valley for the first time.

I felt like giving him everything. I looked at him. His smooth face was tanned already from his long days outside.

"You're the sexiest person I know too," I said quietly.

But he recoiled. I knew it though his expression did not change; I could feel it in my heart, which began to dart about in sudden fear, like the rats when they first realized they were inside a gas chamber.

"Look, I'm an asshole," he said. "Why do you like me so much?"

Then the comforting treetops around the meadow blurred and froze, became foreign and absurd. I wanted to be gone. I wanted to float away. I wanted the light and the wind and the nothingness.

"Why don't you want me to like you?" I had to ask.

"I don't . . . . Look, I don't care. Like me if you want to. If you had any respect for yourself you wouldn't."

I turned away from him, trying to regain myself. I couldn't look at the sky anymore, so big and hopeless.

Now I was staring at the blurry outline of a mosquito

twitching in the web of a spider, close to my face in the grass, and I tried to focus my mind around it, like that small disconnected image was the reason why I'd come.

The web was intricately fantastic and round, like a dream the little black spider had woven in the air to dazzle its victims. And the spider had just caught what it wanted. But now it danced across the silk rungs to its prey, and as it wound the prey rapidly in the material of the web, round and round and round, I saw it destroy the design completely. The dream pattern crumpled and collapsed around the thing it had dreamed for, and I saw the empty air and the ugliness of fulfillment.

"Never mind," he said. "I just got back from a trip. It's Friday. Let's go back and get drunk."

We did.

And so did all the others in the lounge, in the light of lamps and candles that night. I lost him to the crowd again, and I knew that moment in the valley had been lost to the realm of faraway winters. Though it was the valley where my shadow had led me, as if by magic.

That was the day I learned that coincidence doesn't mean anything. Or at least, it doesn't mean what you want it to mean about the future. Because beauty is a rhythm outside of time.

But when I drank that fire it made me say, out loud to anyone who would hear me,

"I'm lonely here."

The beautiful lynx girl was sitting beside me, somehow. Did she work here? In that smooth and perfect way in which (I later found out) she achieved all social interaction, she leaned over and said loudly,

"You should fuck *him*."

I laughed nervously. "Never," I said, bluffing.

He'd heard us. I saw him look down with that secret, self-satisfied smile. He looked down at his lap, his groin, with his smug lips pressed together.

When I looked at his face I saw that he already knew I was his. I couldn't believe I would indeed sleep with him that night. Neither hurt nor love would stop me.

Could I ever be so certain as he was right then? I mean about anything, let alone another person.

There were ways we could not touch.

It's hard to explain. I could touch any part of him. I could be as wild as I wanted to. I could fuck him as hard as I wanted to, in any position—if I wanted to.

But there were ways my hands could not linger. There were places on his face I could not kiss, and moments of hesitation I could not prolong.

Maybe I was superstitious, but I believed that if I made these motions I would give something away. He would sense my tenderness like a predator smells weakness. He would know that in my heart I was breaking the rules.

"I have to stop getting drunk or I'll keep coming in here."

"Why won't you come in here when you're sober?"

"Because it's bad."

"Why?"

"Because."

"Because I'll get emotionally attached."

"Right."

"I promise I won't."

"You can't promise. Girls can't not get emotionally attached."

"Why are you so scared of what I might feel for you?"

He looked away and I swallowed. I had said too much again. I felt the abyss rising up like the inside of darkness.

"I don't want to belong to anyone," he said, and the lightness was gone from his voice. "I don't want to have some relationship that has to be named and defined."

"Right," I said, trying to pull him back with my mind the way I tried to focus the raptors' attention with my love. "It's just a feeling in the moment. No commitment."

"But I don't even know what I feel in the moment. I don't want to have to name that either."

I thought of the moment on the lake, the absolution of nothingness. Freedom.

But I also thought about love.

I've known other loves since this one.

I've known cold windy loves and sweet hot loves. I've known loves I felt in my fingers, and whose ache I felt in the weight of my breasts. Loves that cradled me and loves that brewed a homemade joy in my gut.

I've known loves that necessitated touch, and loves that were too beautiful to touch. Loves that owned me and loves that freed me. Loves that built me up with tears and tore me down with laughter.

Best friend loves and sister loves and brother loves. Loves that rolled me in summer fields and lay me down to rest, and loves that thrilled me like running up a hill on a cold winter morning and shouting out loud when I reached the top. Loves that lingered like a sore throat, and loves I took slowly on my tongue to heal me—and to make the feeling last.

I mean it's true you want something from everyone you love. Sometimes you want to make prettily wrapped gifts for them, and for them to take those gifts and be warmed. Or you want their admiration, or at least a piece of their respect.

Or you want them to lie down behind you, one hand resting on your hip, breathing under your hair.

Or you want them to listen to your life and love every part of its art.

Or you want them to press you against the wall in some instant and want you back beyond all reason.

Or you want them to ask you a great favor, so you can prove your love.

Or you want them to walk with you on some damp night in the forest, whispering.

Is there one perfect love? Is there one love where all you want is one person's eternal and utter dedication?

I don't know. I began with the boy. I began with wanting a love that could not be given.

I began with the perfection of a love that never was.

SUMMER

And in this lies my honour and my reward,—
That whenever I come to the fountain to drink I find the
living water itself thirsty;
And it drinks me while I drink it.

-Kahlil Gibran

*F*awn in the grass. She is earth and grass, swimming in shadow, swimming in stillness. She is the breeze and the silence. She has no smell. She is nothing.

Her mother moves in the meadow, slow and aware, pretending she is alone—pretending there has never been the gush of blood and birth that was the fawn's beginning only hours before.
The fawn lies perfectly still like nothing, while the doe guards without appearing to guard, watches without appearing to watch. The fawn's only job is not to be anything, not to appear.

She is invisible. And invisible, she is everything. She is the hum of the clouds across space, and the hum of the wind through the contours of the grasses, and the hum of the earth with insects, and the ripple of the leaves, and even the moving prints of the sun on her own dappled back through the thicket. Her body becomes the pattern of the world.

Days pass. The mother moves always nearby, a warm anchor.

The fawn is beginning to differentiate the rhythms of the leaves. She feels the casual lift and fall, leaning to and fro of the leaves in the wind—a motion with no defined beginning or end, a motion that flows over time, always changing and never appearing to change.

Then there are the moments. There are the interruptions in space—there is a rustle that means an animal is moving. The sudden blurt of sound that is the mark of a living being, a life condensed into one moment in the felt pattern of eternity.

The two kinds of sound are different—one soothing, one sudden; one whole, one partial; one boundless, one bound.

There is a difference between these two languages the leaves speak: the language of the wind with its ongoing everythingness, and the language of animals—which hunger and hide, strive and fear, kill and die. It is the most important difference she will ever learn. It is the difference that makes her real. It is the separation.

Through it she begins to sense the motion of the predator.

She feels his nose nuzzling the earth longingly after her yet unborn scent. She feels the smooth burst of his energy, his tireless trot through hidden tunnels of shadow, under the slant of fallen trees, along the leaf-strewn forest pathways he has known forever, at the boundary between forest and sky-covered meadow, along the edges of her mother's field of vision. She feels his hunger. She feels it in her bones, her sharp legs, her new organs, her open eyes. She feels her own body.

Everything she is made of understands this hunger. And it is through his hunger that she begins to understand what she is.

Eight

We were all out of gas for killing the rats. I would have to kill them by slinging them against the countertop and smashing their skulls.

"I can't do it," I told him. "Please, do it for me."

"I don't want to do it. It's your job. If you don't do it, the raptors will just go hungry."

"I can't," I repeated. "Please."

"Why? Why can't you?"

"Because of . . . how it affects me. It's painful. I don't know how to explain."

"Well maybe it affects me too. Did you ever think of that?" He was yelling. "Why the hell do you have to get so emotional? It's ridiculous."

"This is how I live," I said, beginning to cry because I could not bear to be yelled at, and because I had no choices then. "I live my life with emotion."

That seemed true. I felt beautiful suddenly. So beautiful I seemed to burn a hole in the air. The tears rounding my cheekbones seemed to come not from my eyes but from a rain far above me, and I could feel the heave of my throat and the taut line of my clavicle and the proud softness of my breasts beneath the downpour.

He looked away.

"Fine," he said. He began to put on his boots, cursing me. "Let's go. I will kill one goddamned rat."

We stomped out into the rain and the night, and I felt the weight of his boots in my stomach. My body drank in the heat of his body beside mine, but it was like poison, full of fury. How I longed for walks in the night with him. How I longed for the darkness dissolving our forms next to each other. But this was not what I longed for.

"Emotions are useless," he said, walking fast. "They have no evolutionary purpose."

I thought about this, but I couldn't think of any argument to the contrary.

Inside the shed he made me pick out a rat from one of the cages. I was shaking. I handed him one, any one. It was a female, was all I knew.

When he slung her against the countertop the first time, her head broke into a shatter of blood. But she was still writhing—writhing like they never did all those times I opened the gas chamber and peeked inside for long moments, shyly praying. So he slung her against the counter again and this time the blood splashed all onto the walls.

I realized he didn't really know how to do it, and I wondered guiltily if he'd ever done it before. He slammed the body down again, and I think even a fourth time, but by this time I wasn't aware of much. Except for the shaking of his hands.

I felt so sorry. For him.

And I knew he was right, too. This was the real killing. This was nature.

"Thank you," I said when he was done, not wiping away the marks of my tears.

"That's all I'm doing," he said dully. "There's some frozen meat in the freezer, I think. Road kill we got donated, stuff like that. You should know. You do work here, don't you?"

"I'm sorry," I said weakly, "It's like you said . . . girls are crazy, right?"

"No," he answered as he washed his hands. "I would say that you're crazy because you're a girl. But that's not it. I know other girls, and they at least sometimes make some sense."

Then to my surprise he looked at me hard, as if expecting me to answer him.

And I suddenly felt that he wanted something from me, too, but I didn't know how to give it.

After he left, I washed the blood off the walls, and fed the raptors in a daze. I was still shaking as I washed the meat smell off my hands and went to the tank of the black rat snake. We fed the snakes live rats. But I wanted to hold her before I fed her. I didn't think about how to approach her. I just reached in and rolled her into my hands before either of us knew what was happening.

I carried her, one cold loop in each hand, into the other room, and lay her down on the table. I expected her to leap into freedom, to unspool across the open surface like fire. But she lay still and nervously flicked her tongue. I touched her, and watched the silent fountain inside me—that welling nausea which was need, which was fear, the fear of needing—subside.

Then I touched my own skin—the skin of my throat and the heat between my breasts and over my belly—and I began to feel safe again. And I was comforted by the touch, again, of the snake, and the feel of me—me that there was, just touching.

It is just me, I thought, as if with relief. This is all I can be.

I lifted the snake again and she tasted my sweat, rounded my elbow, looked for a dark place. I was a cradle for her body, a warm touch and a scent, and that was all.

I returned her to the tank, and then I picked a baby rat out of one of the cages to feed to her. I felt helpless as I dropped its little twist of a body into her cage. *I don't understand life*, I thought, *so I give it to you—to do with it what you will.*

I had never seen a snake eat before. Usually I had to leave the rat in there, letting the snake get around to her killing in her own time. But tonight she was slinking toward it already as I withdrew my hand. She approached it with her tongue flaming at it, her metallic eyes focused deceptively on some non-existent horizon. The rat did not see her but went to the corner and moved uneasily there, as if it knew. I watched, mesmerized, for I did not know. I did not understand, really.

I was not prepared for the relief I felt when the snake's mouth snapped around that body and hushed its quivering fear.

I was not prepared for the comfort I felt in watching the embrace of those jaws, or the sudden peace of the rat, who had lived the whole of its brief life in anxiety and ceaseless trembling.

I watched the snake tuck her snout into the folds of the rat's skin, and nestle into the fur, rolling her flat head and opening her flat dark grin with a sensuous and ecstatic surrender. I watched the soft flexibility of those hard scales as she engulfed the flesh, savoring it, as the flesh of the rat in turn seemed to bunch tenderly against her delicate skull. And the scales wrinkled like cloth, and the pink pointed toes trembled with perfection, and the skin of the snake rollicked and undulated with joy over the design of the rat, and the rat traveled the long tunnel to heaven via the beautiful pathway of the snake's body.

I watched those two bodies slide inside each other, my wrists pressed lightly against the edges of the tank, as if bound.

I walked back to my cabin in a thick darkness, in the silence after rain. By the time I intuited the open space of the trail somehow, and turned into it, a new world was opening—a misty, uncertain world steamed off a brew of black nothing. A world too young and innocent to be feared.

A puffy, lightless light, simmering up between the lilies and the moon, gathered moistly the sensations of my eyes and skin. I could see the layers of the forest in every direction, and the stars falling all into them, and the distant hum of the lake's reflections.

At the end of the hollow space that was the main trail, I could see specks of light, and those were the cabins.

My cabin seemed so unimportant then, a little flea upon the beast of infinity—and all the little sorrows and obsessions inside it, equally pointless.

The next morning I walked to the shed slowly.

When aspens are young, their trunks glow an unearthly green, like swamp ghosts.

Young birches glow a pungent pink, like blood running beneath white skin.

I held the delicacy of morning color like lace in my vision—watched the way it decorated the summer light.

I came to the shed door. I was afraid.

A funny thing had happened. The power had gone out in the killing room.

When I flicked the light switch, nothing happened.

I stood in the doorway and listened to the broken rhythm of the rats shuffling in the dark: their sounds cut off at the ends, like questions. They knew I was there. They wondered.

I stood still in the comfortable place of indecision. There were the raptors who needed to eat, whom I loved, who knew nothing of a civilized human's fear of killing. There were the rats who did not want to be killed, who were smart and lived communally. There was the boy, whom I could not face, and I, who had tried for so long to be invisible, and yet longed so deeply to be seen.

Then I saw the note on the door. The boy had gone to the store to buy gas.

Grateful and guilty, I turned to go. I would feed them later when we had the gas—that quiet, unfrightening death. But I felt the horrid stifling darkness behind me and turned around again. I knew it didn't really matter, objectively, that the rats had never felt sunlight in their lives. But it made me sad, emotional human that I was.

There were about twenty cages, and with each one I carried out to the deck, I felt a little bolder and a little less foolish. When they were all laid out in the aliveness of that particular sunny day (*What day was it? What grand, important, real-life things were happening in the world that day?*), I squatted down and watched their curious noses twitch against the mesh roofs of their cages. I felt joy—the kind that weighs nothing, that doesn't depend on anyone or on any tangible thing.

Maybe compassion has no purpose, I thought. Maybe it has no sense. Maybe coincidence, the moment when he appears just as you were thinking his name, means nothing at all about what will happen or what is meant to happen. Maybe all that matters is this moment, and the gesture you make.

And it is better if the gesture is beautiful.

Not better for you or even better for the whole ecosystem necessarily. Just better. Better the way the sunlight is better than a closed room.

He breezed by in the afternoon, returning from his lone Saturday wanderings.

"Want to go for a canoe ride?" he asked, without looking at me. What was that challenge ever-present in his voice? If I'd brought it up, he would have mocked me.

We heard the first loon call of the season together that day. We were alone in the middle of the lake again. I remembered the winter day he'd paused there and understood with me, for a moment, the silence. But I knew he would not remember such a moment.

"I'm sorry I was a jerk last night," he said all of the sudden. "About killing the rats." He was paddling slowly, almost hesitantly. I watched the long lonely stride of his muscles in front of me, fascinated. I couldn't believe what I'd heard.

"I was in a bad mood that day. I just needed some time alone," he said, and the idea of his absence all day, the spring woods vibrant with his mysterious boy passage, flashed through my hips like pain. "I feel better now. I was just in a bad mood." He laughed nervously. "So I took it out on you."

I waited. I could not see his face, nor could he see mine. But I felt as if he were handing me some small frail thing. Something more alive than any of my tears or imagined suffering. Something that would never survive evolution.

"So I hope you'll forgive me," he added. And he looked out

to the water in a dreaming sort of way for just a moment, like maybe he really did hope that.

I held the fragile thing in my hands, this thing I might be able to keep.

"It's fine," I said, treading gently. "Thank you."

But I watched the closed motion of his muscles, and I was thinking and thinking, wanting more. Reflections passed under the boat and disappeared. From the side I saw his face pressed back into that comfortable firmness again, his lips so tight I thought his teeth must be clenched beneath them. I caressed that gift he gave me, but I knew he would no longer seem to care.

After the moment died down, dried up and blew away, I said:

"How can I talk to you, so that you won't hurt me?"

Silence.

"I mean . . . why are you like that? Why do you mock me?"

Maybe if I treated him gently, he would be gentle. Maybe if I trusted him, he would become worthy of trust.

He kept paddling ahead of me, like his body knew its function instinctually, its endless push and pull with the world.

"Because you're weak," he said off-handedly. "It's only natural."

Of course. There is no forgiveness in nature. And it was a weakness, wasn't it, to swoon before beauty? To neglect all work and function sometimes for the helpless pleasure of a long contemplation by the lake? Wasn't love a weakness? And the way I wanted to lie down in the earth like an animal and disappear? Wasn't it?

"Hey, steer us over to that island."

I tried to respond quickly, angling us over to the little bar of sand and mud he had motioned to with his head. I was no good at steering.

"Shh . . . Slow down," he commanded as we rammed up against its small shore. I was still gathering apologies, gathering the flustered feathers of my thoughts, when I realized he didn't really care. He was pointing at a tiny, sand-colored bird that ran like an ant along the length of the bar.

"See, it's a killdeer," he said interestedly, "and she's got a nest."

I watched the bird run, and then suddenly change her behavior completely. She was performing an act I'd only read about, flopping along in a lopsided pathetic way, away from us, faking a broken wing. She had a nest she was trying to distract us from.

"Okay, okay, we're following you, we're following you, you're so wounded," the boy said teasingly to the bird, and pushed the canoe up a little with the edge of his paddle. I loved his unacknowledged respect for her, and the urgency of his curiosity as he followed her, and the sound of his voice talking to something so small. I laughed in spite of myself.

Somewhere in the tiny bit of grass there, the killdeer must have eggs, or even babies, no bigger than my thumb. But she was so good at her act—so believable, so attractively grotesque, so interesting. Acting out a little drama of pain and suffering to distract us from what was so simple, vulnerable, and real in some hidden space nearby.

My mind fell quiet then, for once, and searched among the still patches of grass, wondering.

The raccoon rises up on his haunches, holding tight to the fish he has just caught. He can feel its life surge into his hands like a fever and then extinguish forever. He smiles in his belly. He has the world in his hands.

But now for just a moment he is watching a figure move downstream. It is a big thing, but it moves like a small thing—forward and back, light on its feet, bending and shrinking in the light. Like a deer, but not a deer—too abrupt in its motions, unbalanced, seeming helpless, like something in so much pain that it cannot attune itself to its surroundings.

Ah, but now he catches its scent—just a little breeze of it over the river. Human. He drops to three sturdy paws, clasping the fish to his chest with the fourth, and runs for cover. But at the mouth of the shadows, he turns and glances back.

The human is so interesting. It does not seem quite human. It has been still now for several moments, and seems to confuse itself with the stones and the river and even the voices of the fish that the raccoon heard with his hands when he dipped them into the water. The human is such a curious confusion of parts. It could be so many things. Yet it seems unable to decide.

I hardly even tried to write anymore. Instead, I began to take trails I'd never taken.

Once, having only just come from the cages and still sniffing my hands with a morbid fascination for the smell of death, I came to a small river.

When I knelt by the white water I saw it break into hundreds of fish.

They streamed up the current and hurled themselves up the falls against merciless gravity. I was close enough to touch the slick of their rosy, writhing backs, softer than the inside of my mouth.

I watched and watched, my focus fading in and out.

It became tiring, watching them fall back down again and again, dashed against the rocks and unable to rest before the next attempt without getting swept meters backward.

At last, unable to control myself, I reached out and grabbed a fish. It was almost easy; there were so many of them. I tossed it into the current high above the little falls, grateful that its struggle was finally over—that I had found a way to love one small thing.

But to my horror the fish lay still when it hit the higher water, as if shocked. And then, first slowly and then with speed, the water carried it all the way back down the falls. It did not start writhing again until it had fallen way behind the others.

I thought then about the look in the owl's eyes when I tried to tell her about love.

I thought, I've made a mistake. For the animals there are only two things: life and death. There is no purgatory of emotion in between—no strange empty place of wanting things to be different than they are.

So my gesture had meant nothing. I stood up and walked away.

The Great-horned Owl in his cage, hungry, clacking his beak.

His eyes too black, too big for the cage. His urges, his needs, his fears so much simpler than mine. So much easier to act on.

Maybe today I would not try to be a tree, or a shadow, or nothing. I would not try to shrink invisibly into and out of the cage as if I could belong there. I would just be myself.

I would weigh my fear, and present it honestly.

This is me, with my heavy bones and detailed face, with my ignorance and gracelessness, entering the cage not hiding my vulnerability. This is my complex and frightened humanity.

I faced him, lifting my wrist, and felt my heart open.

He clasped my wrist, bound it with his toes, saw me.

He did not love me. He still clacked his beak, stared at me with a wary wildness in his one good eye, hated me or feared me. But something happened. I felt some brush of his presence, a small grey breath, pass through me. As if he'd said something.

It had a certain flavor to it, a certain texture—like a whim I might have felt in some daydreaming moment long ago, when I was a child.

The boy told me I would have to take his place tomorrow evening. I would have to teach his wildlife signs class for him because he would be involved in an important research project that night. He and his new assistant would be netting and tagging the loons. It was part of a study about the effects of pollution in the lake.

He told me this in the dining hall at the long wooden table, with children and adults all around, shouting to each other like crows. He looked at me levelly as he told me: it was a challenge.

"So you'll have to teach for me," is what he said.

"Fine," I said, knowing I didn't have the guts to question his authority. I knew he knew I was afraid.

"You think you can do it?" he said. "It's a three-hour class. You have to take them on a hike and not get lost."

"Can you give me some materials or something?" I asked, wondering why people value strength and courage so much more highly than gentleness.

"I don't use any materials," he said. "I just make it up as I go along."

"Well fine, good for you."

"Fine, good for you," he mocked in a high, tremulous voice.

"What?" I demanded suddenly, leaning toward his face. "You don't think I can teach your class? You don't think I'll be good at it?"

He looked back at me with equal suddenness, his eyes moving and brightening like the sun emerging in pieces from behind the clouds, and the corners of his mouth lifted just a little. But then he looked away.

"Calm down," he said. "I didn't say that. I just want you to do it."

I took a walk in the morning, when the light was weightless, and the restless grasses by the marsh turned the color of bananas.

I stood quietly and listened to my breath. I wanted to teach the children to love beauty. I wanted them to see the yellow sun shaking through the turning grasses and to know about being alive.

I wanted, at the very least, to move them with one small thing.

Because I knew that even in elementary school, they were already lonely. And someday, if they were good at living, they would realize that they were lonely. And what then?

I wanted to teach the children to lay down their hands in an animal's tracks, to learn the dance of another being. To learn the questions and motives of another animal with the strings of their own muscles, the stretched cells of their own skin, the friction of their own joints. To learn empathy.

I knelt to look at something strange and ugly near my knees, and found the empty husk of a dragonfly larva like a little monster in the grass. I loved again to discover this miracle, though I'd discovered it many times that summer—to see the ghost image of this lowly crawling thing, clinging to a blade of grass on the brink of flight as if it could never have been anything else, and to know that it had disappeared into the air with its wings of fire after all, as if anything could happen, at any time.

I wanted to show the children this. I wanted to show them miracles.

But before those city creatures I would appear stark and helpless as a deer in a daylit street. I had no language.

The lynx girl, with her long graceful spine and her snow-drift hair, smiled across at the boy.

He was teaching her different types of loon calls.

He played a tape recording. This is the yodel, he said, the territorial call that only the male makes. This is the wail, the sound they use to call each other. He mimicked it irreverently, like a baby whining. She laughed.

It turned out she was his new assistant. She would be the one. She would be the one to learn from him, listen dutifully to his words, worship the confidence of his voice.

This is the tremolo, he said. The territorial call that both sexes make.

Where was I in this scene? In a corner, in the shadow: pale, almost transparent, thin and hungry.

Her face was freckled and cheerful. She was so normal, so easy. Freckled and laughing. Such an easy self to express.

She listened the way he wanted someone to listen, loving everything he said. And not needing him to say anything more.

I came down to the valley of foxes, fresh and alive with summer.

I waited and waited but I never saw them. I had never seen them.

Still, this was my haven of red valentine sumac and green freedoms and shifting light. I told myself I did not care about the normal, easy girl who, no matter how many moments of laughter she shared with the boy, would never come here.

What did her longing look like? Not like this.

Here came the children of the city.

They came yelling and kicking at the door of that strange and foggy sanctuary which was myself, my presence in this world. They came knocking at the door of my senses, expectant and demanding, not seeing me.

I led them along trails that they only perceived by their dim resemblance to roads. And they pushed to get ahead, complaining of mosquitoes, not knowing where they were pushing to. Pushing past each other, pushing past everything I would have led them here to see. *Where are you going?* I wanted to ask them, but at the same time I did not care. Now I just wanted this to be over. They were a different species from me, and I would never understand them.

But I took them all the way to the beaver lodge, where the yellow grasses sighed like lovers. I told them how beavers are the only other mammals that change their habitat to suit them. But the children only stared at me or threw sticks in the water, and I realized I did not know how to explain why that fact seemed important to me.

I did not know where I could take them that would speak to them as it spoke to me; I did not know what to do with them.

I thought of where I would run to when this was over. It was almost dusk now, and the foxes in the red valley would be busy with their subtle, quiet work, listening with their big ears against the ground to hear the movements of worms and grubs, and scenting the wake of the mice in the grass. I would go there and be very quiet with them, and let the night finger my hair, and be soothed.

But then I thought of the boy, standing there at the beaver lodge with me, and how he'd told me he didn't want to be analyzed or picked apart or forced to be anything. He'd just moved like a fleeting fox from one small amazement to the next. He'd just given me what he could in each moment. And he wouldn't have stopped to ponder whether or not I was the right person to see a certain place that amazed him.

"I know a secret place," I told them. And began walking.

I couldn't notice all the things the boy could notice, while so aware of the children behind and around me, and what I looked like to them. I wondered now why I had to work so hard to find the ease the boy found in every moment, why I had to struggle so poignantly for deep connection when he seemed already so seamlessly connected with his surroundings that every scent and track called to him.

But tonight, for me, the foxes appeared.

The children were suddenly, amazingly silent.

Ah, so nature is real, they seemed to tell themselves. The tracks were real. They hushed each other, stared, pointed anxiously as if each were the only one who saw them.

Four fox babies playing, looking bewildered, looking at us, lifting their paws absentmindedly—here where I alone had seen only silver rings of hair and scattered bones.

For that moment everything that was precious to me was safe. The moment stayed intact. Everything respected everything else.

A little boy asked me, "Are they afraid of us?"

And another asked, "How did you know they would be here?"

Some of the children were looking at me now, and I was looking at the foxes. And in the foxes I saw the children. I saw that they were not so different from me. I saw that their souls, too, were made of wonder.

What made the foxes appear now, like a blessing? What made them come now, after all the weeks I'd wandered here alone wishing to see them, stalking them and lying respectfully, silently, in the grass waiting—what made them appear now, for no reason, before all these noisy children?

The sky seemed to laugh and lean low, brushing my cheek. The grass shimmered up to the fading sun in ecstasy. The wind strode through the trees toward us.

Maybe after you love something for a long time, it will come to you after all. But only at the right moment. And only on its own terms.

Like a gift. Like compassion.

Only when you make some gesture to share the beauty that is yours.

Only when you are willing to accept what is. Only when you are willing to give something up.

$\sim$

I took the children back to a clearing at the edge of the woods—between the woods and the building where they would have noise again, and the numb cushion of humanity, and food whose origins they would never think of—and I asked them to draw close to me and listen.

I spoke to them in the quiet way that my voice felt most comfortable, hardly more than a whisper.

"You see," I told them, "we humans, we move through the woods so loudly, and everything around us hides and seems silent. But you saw those foxes. And if you think about it, you know that there are actually thousands and even millions of animals—if you count every bird and insect too—in this forest right now, living their lives without us even hearing them. The forest looks quiet and still, but a whole world is happening—living and dying and being born again, right here, right around us, while we hear nothing."

The children's eyes were wide and their listening was like a warm, restless gift they laid hopefully down before me in the center of the circle. Like a newborn animal.

And my voice, wherever it came from, sounded like a river: smooth and easy and as old as water itself. It didn't even sound like mine—any more than the foxes were mine, or the forest, or the wind.

And I wondered then if beauty was not a weight I had to bear alone after all, but rather the thing that saved me, at the last minute, from my own humanness.

Walking back to my cabin I could already see the future.

There would be my empty room, whose thick loneliness I would lie down inside and rest—to the light music of fantasy.

Or if I were very lucky, there would be the real boy in my arms tonight, and the depth of hot otherness in which to lose my weary self, but only for a very short time.

Or—and this was the most likely possibility—there would be the agony between. Neither aloneness nor togetherness, but the moment of habitual pain when I would walk into the dining hall and see him turn away from me, or hear his mocking laughter, or feel his teasing touch followed by the wind of his leaving.

Inside me, there would be the high of his presence and the fall of his absence.

And that nothingness in between, neither life nor death—only a purgatory of wanting.

There would be me begging for something he would not give—would not even acknowledge. There would be me loving him for some beauty he would never admit to, and him hurting me over and over, because he did not want to be loved.

Was this a good story?
Was this, really, a story I wanted to tell?

"I want to talk to you," I said.

It was a bad moment for it, I knew. And in the office, of all places. But no one else was there, besides us.

I was returning the magnifying glasses and the animal furs I had borrowed to teach his class, and he was photocopying something, and he had asked me in that challenging way, *Well? How did it go?* And I had been able to answer with pride.

But now I was afraid of how long I would have to wait

before I saw him again. I watched his thumbs skim the surface of the photocopier buttons, trying to find the one he wanted; I watched the hands which were ugly to my eyes, but not to my body.

"So can I talk to you—I mean really talk to you?" My heart was huge and heavy. I felt I could just barely keep him, like he was some elusive memory I had to use all my energy to keep in focus.

"What?" came his sudden anger. "Just say it!"

"Well okay . . . ." But I was terrified now. "Remember how you said . . . that I didn't respect myself if I liked you . . . when you said . . ."

"I don't want to talk about this."

"But you don't know what I'm going to say," I protested.

"I don't care. I don't want to have this conversation. God, I don't understand this fucking thing. Do you know how to copy double-sided?"

"Listen to me. I just want to be real with you. I feel like I can never talk to you."

"Don't talk to me then. We just won't talk."

He turned and faced me, his arms swinging awkwardly from his shoulders like his body was a joke we were both embarrassed about.

"I'm an asshole, okay? I've told you that. I'm an asshole. Get used to it."

I looked at him. "That's a terrible excuse," I said.

He grinned. I tried not to, but then I did too.

"I hate you," I heard one of us say helplessly. It was me.

"I love you," he said tiredly. "Let's get married and have children." And he grabbed his copies from the machine, looking suddenly vulnerable with his crumpled handful of pages like the half-done homework of a little boy, and walked out.

On my way home that night, the raccoon man called to me. I didn't want to stop so I just waved and kept going, but he called again.

"Don't I even get a hello?"

I turned around. He was smiling, and I felt suddenly on the verge of tears. But I had the strange thought that I had been selfish with myself by walking by. That I had hurt someone with my own hurt. I came slowly toward him, and felt the tears ball up in my throat and clamp tight. I couldn't look at him.

"I'm sorry," I said.

"Hey, it's okay. Do you want some fish?"

I looked at the meat he was frying in his pan.

"Where did you get it?" I asked politely, because somehow casual conversation seemed like the only thing possible anymore.

"I caught it."

"You did?" Some unexpected curiosity stepped up inside me.

"Yeah. Millions of them swimming upriver right now. You ever seen them?"

"Oh!" I said. "I did see them once. The salmon."

"Alewives," he corrected me, but when I looked at his face there was no smugness there. In fact there seemed a strange sort of gratitude in his eyes. I sat down.

Then he began to talk, as he always did, and I began to drift away, the way I knew how to do.

He was talking about fishing maybe, or some other thing. My heart meandered listlessly up the dome of the sky, perched itself in a cloud, and looked down on him dully with its chin on its knees.

But at some point he handed me a plate of fish, and I had to accept it somehow, because it felt too lonely not to.

And maybe it was because I hadn't tasted meat in so long, but when I took a bite of the fish I had another funny thought—that I had never really noticed eating before. Now

I noticed it. I noticed the transformed flesh of an animal surrendering to the flesh of my tongue, and the way my taste buds rose to meet it, and the way the saliva flooded into my mouth gently in welcome. When I swallowed it, I swallowed life and wildness, and the knowing in the dependable hands of the raccoon man as he dipped them in the cold hysteria of the river.

And then I found he was saying something strange to me.

He was saying, "But what are you really thinking about, as I'm sitting here talking at you?"

And now I watched my heart immediately stand up and begin to walk down from the clouds. It was only now that I perceived what a really long distance it was. It took so long for me to come down.

But I did, and he waited, and then I told him. My voice came from out of my throat where his wild fish had gone, and rolled over my tongue.

I told him something I was really thinking. I told him about the boy and how there was nothing I could do to be at peace with him.

"It doesn't matter if I'm kind. He still hurts me," I said.

"Why do you wish that it were different?" the raccoon man said. "Why do you need it to be a certain way?"

The world was so quiet, so simple in this moment—I remember. I could still taste my own words, like I could taste the fish. And every sound I could hear—the occasional birdsong, the unknown rustling, the wind waking the brown leaves on the trail—became the sound of my listening. Sorrow made me so simple.

I realized this man was calm and easy, in a universe where I could find no rest.

"It just seems wrong . . ." I fumbled.

"Is it wrong when the wolf kills the fawn? When the owl kills the rabbit?"

I thought for a little while. Yes, I had seen the snake make love to the rat in devouring it; I had seen that rightness. I thought of my longing for the animal. To be flesh and earth. To finally know my place that perfectly, and never to doubt myself again. I remembered grabbing a living thing from the river with my raw human hand, instead of just giving in to the way things were.

But I also remembered the beauty of giving the rats the sunlight.

"It's different," I said. "People are different. We can change the pattern. We can play different roles." And then I added, "We can love."

"Ah," he said, looking at me slyly. "So you know what love is then?"

And I didn't say anything, because now that someone asked me, I wasn't sure.

Again that night I felt the necessity of the boy in the dark, my body like an ocean of creatures that rose to the surface for feeding.

The power he wielded. The shape of his grin on my neck. The long stroke of his finger flickering under the rim of my underwear, and his words made only of breath,

"Tell me you want me."

I straddled him, pressed his body into the softness that made it helpless, and pressed my lips to his forehead.

"I want you," I whispered, feeling scared because I knew it wasn't how he wanted me to say it. *Do you want me physically . . . or more than that?* he'd asked me long ago. No don't worry—no more than this. No more than our human flesh, which is everything. No more than my body writing out my wanting now in the ink of slow touch upon all the forbidden places.

The places he forbid me were not between his legs but in the shadows of his face, in the hard silence of his torso, in the warmth upon his throat, and in the unadmitted tightness of his embrace. I lingered in those places now when I was not supposed to, and began to write my story of wanting in a language of spring wind and salt water . . .

"What are you doing?" he said, twisting to push me beneath him again.

But in the silence afterward, I loved his weakness. I loved the weak moments when he was too tired yet to rise, when he lay his head on my breasts, when he had not yet gathered the strength to close himself off to me again.

This, too, was part of the story, and this is why I loved it.

It was like we cancelled each other out. Like positive and negative. It felt so good to be dissolved.

I spent so much time trying to perfect myself, to be worthy of the world. And when he fucked me he knocked me down like a tower of cards. And I just lay there, sprawled out and broken, finally and utterly at rest.

We lay there so long, that night, that we became less solid, and I could feel the unconscious warmth of his body leaning into mine while his mind slept. I imagined the pulse of his sleep entering into me in waves, and then it seemed we were under the sea, in the most pleasant darkness. We were two bodies far below the hungriest depths of the sea, deeper than all the turmoil and weight and dying. And we were swaying there, under the billion-year-old sea, at the bottommost bottom—two skeletons, two peaceful lost dreams bumping ever so lightly together in the very slight, eternal sway of the deepest waters.

And in that smoky depth, images seemed almost to form but did not—dreams were almost answered but were not. And I relaxed into the sway, into the deep purple sleep, where nothing ever became anything. I dreamed myself along the intricate terrain of his breath.

I traversed the detailed tunnels of his unfelt feelings.

I fingered the pattern of his presence.

I licked trembling drops of water from the caves of his heart.

I became intensely comfortable with every bend and fit of our bodies together: resting, breathing, twitching occasionally. In the sway I developed a stillness. Not a lazy stillness but a stillness of whirling atoms and infinite possibility. I was aware of every atom. I became aware of the exact weight and tilt, for example, of his head on my breast, and the texture of the warmth in the space between my thigh and his carelessly fallen hand. I became aware of each moment, and I experienced each moment coming and going like a whole lifetime— each moment unique, with its own special layout of breath and unspoken desire.

Then, being aware of every moment so specifically as it arrived, I got caught up by one moment whose feeling seemed to turn my body just a little, so that I would now rest my hand upon his head.

I could feel it already, with my whole body—the pattern of his hair under my palm. And that action, that movement toward warmth.

But the moment caught on something. It was that something which causes regret, and sorrow, and fear, and desire, and that same something for which reason I am not an animal— not anyone but me, alone in the whole universe.

The moment jolted to a halt. And the other moments jumbled to a halt behind it, and collided together, and then that moment shattered.

It was too late now, to lay my hand on his head. Now, because I had stopped to think, I was afraid. And he would know.

And I saw how each moment contains potential, and how looking back or forward upon it from any other moment will never bring the potential back. Now it was no longer quite right, to move toward him at all. So I let the moment go, knowing it now as a moment where I did not follow the impulse of my body.

But now what? Now that I had let go of the desire in my hand, I began to feel it rising in other places. It would not just disappear. Nothing ever disappears, only reforms. I felt it—strongly, yes possessively—in my stomach now. It was shaped like a wooden bowl, that desire—a handmade wooden bowl, empty and worn. And it began to rock in the stillness, until water splashed out of its emptiness, splashed like something magic up into my chest and now all the way down my arms . . .

He moved.

"What?" he said.

"I didn't say anything." My hands were dizzy. I felt I needed to write something down.

"I have to go," he said suddenly, remembering where he was.

He rose up from the bed like another image of himself, for a moment looking down at the creature he just was—the warm sleeper helpless against my breasts—with abject fear. The fear slid his face shut, and the mask of mockery returned.

And he slid a door shut between us.

And the door was my own name, which he spoke as if he did not know it, as he said goodnight and left me.

We are all made of things. The things we love, I guess.

I am made of willow and the silence of books. The sea, the sleeping of bears, and rivers of ants in the spring.

The sticky sound of trees in the wind after an ice storm, like rain peeling off the ground and rising.

Wind storms, night storms, and the sun in my eyes.

The length of a moment, the stately aging of the forest, the circling footprints of rabbits in the cruelest winter, the red opening of the vagina with the sky inside it. The amazing formations of human hair.

Dreams of a princess, bounding long-skirted through fields of yellow, white, and bird-like flowers.

I am made of these things: beauty I have picked up and carried. And now I was also made of this—this boy inside my body.

All my life I am possessed by the people I have loved, and their motions haunt mine. Sometimes I find myself responding to some suggestion with a certain scowl, turning away with a certain ironic jerk of my chin, or walking one moment with my chest pressed forward and hands hooked at my sides just so. And I remind myself of him, without even knowing how I know, and I observe the feeling I felt when I made that gesture. And suddenly I understand, not everything, but a little about the soul that animated that human body—the things it wanted and the tools it used to torture itself.

The dance, supplicating and proud, that it danced with the world, and with me.

It's like that. At night I sweat the memories, and they come dizzy around me, in all their unspeakable colors. And I live with them, in involuntary love.

Because just as it is the woman's body, not the man's, that is built to carry the fruit of union, likewise it is the woman's spirit, not the man's, that is forced to carry the relationship between them. To carry the burden of a beauty which cannot survive on its own.

It terrifies the man. He must avoid her. And he can—he has this freedom, this choice.

I remember this.

I am sitting alone in a hollow by the water. I am always alone.

Acorns begin to fall on my bare legs. He is standing above me when I turn around. He doesn't smile or speak, only continues tossing acorns at me, like a sullen little boy.

I feel like I'm holding that frail thing again, like a heart, though I don't know if it's his or mine. I believe already that for the rest of my life I will long for this moment, when we inhabit the same forest, when his presence looks so hot, close, and possible. My eyes crawl up to him from the ground, pressing between the ridges of his jeans.

I feel like my heart has been assigned to him by some force greater than myself, regardless of the pain it will cause me. I feel like my body has been assigned to his. I feel like love, or whatever this is, is a story unfolding between us that neither of us can control.

Always I will want this. Always.

And I don't even know what it is.

The memories of what he will remember as only fucking float back to me later on, when I am alone.

I remember the way he kissed me one time—slowly, for once, and with wonder—and the way he touched the edge of my lips with his fingers as I kissed him back, as if fascinated that my mouth could so love his.

I remember his almost imperceptible sigh when he kissed my neck the first time, having just entered my bed in the darkness, as if giving in.

I remember the way he once asked me, when inside me—in a voice he would never use with me or with anyone in any other context, in words he would never even admit to at any other time—if he was hurting me, if I was okay.

Or this.

I am laying down my journal for the night, about to undress. I jump and turn at a rapping on my window. On his way off to some late-night wandering, he has stopped in the darkness, a bright-eyed ghoul against the glass, and now he is waggling his tongue at me and laughing. I am flattered somehow. I saunter up to the window and lick the glass.

He grins quietly, and I thrill to bring out the shyness in a loud wild boy, the way one thrills to bring out the wildness in someone shy. Perhaps more so. I say boldly,

"Shall I undress for you?"

He shrugs. "If you want."

But it isn't enough for me—this reply. I turn off the light, full of pride and insecurity, and he walks away into his world.

I go to bed alone, imagining that the white trilliums still bloom.

The raccoon man is so kind. He offers to read me a story one night. I even allow myself to lie down on his bench and look up at the stars while he reads it.

He opens a book and reads from something called the "Heart Sutra." He reads something I can't remember, except I know it has to do with transcending the cycles of suffering—the suffering we bring upon ourselves again and again, in a thousand million lives over.

It comforts me.

When I get up he pats me on the shoulder, lightly, his big hand respecting and avoiding the heat of my body.

"Don't worry so much," he says. And then he goes inside his cabin, leaving me alone.

When I lie down to sleep that night, my heart lies down with me in gratitude. I am content and warm. I fold myself into my covers and close my eyes, snuggling and smiling to myself.

Half into a dream I think fondly, *He is kind but he doesn't know how it is. He doesn't know that I cherish my suffering, that it makes my life worth living. Suffering is the shadow of longing.*

I don't know if I could ever let that go.

I don't know if I could ever be different than I am.

I lay awake—in the absence of the boy; in the presence of longing. I threaded my mind along the thin line of a mosquito's whine in the dark.

A mosquito begins as a dream attached to the possibility of water. It is a dream its mother had before she died, leaving it egg-bound on some shore of mud sweetened with decay.

Over the long winter it divides unthinkingly into perfect segments, extending into a creature with beginning and end. The instinctual plans of its future line up in order: the underwater, the air, the blood, the dance.

In human time, the mosquito's life is hardly more than a moment. It is a life condensed into such intensity that it consists of nothing but a singular frenzy of desire. It is an utterly mortal life.

But before that life begins, there is the long winter, and then there is a time of harmless floating, where the mosquito is only a minute scribble on the surface of a puddle—not even aware of the difference between itself and any random piece of forest debris.

It emerges from the egg, a question inspired by the opening of some small shadowed pool to summer.

It rises in the loose balloon of liquid, and hooks onto the surface—the line between the underwater and the air.

Only the larva knows this: that the line in between—between lightness and darkness, between life and death—is a world in itself. A world that twitches just slightly when the breeze passes over it.

Anything could destroy this creature—this tiniest of lives—which is barely a creature yet at all. It does not know itself. It churns anything and everything into its mouth, which is not even really a mouth but some inchoate opening. It does not seek or even wait for fulfillment; the world is constantly there.

But there are times when it must struggle. There are times when water droplets fall like stones from above, and it must convulse frantically to maintain contact with the air which is its breath. For even something so tiny still breathes—and this, too, amazes me.

What is it like to pass over from water to air? What did the first creature ever to tip its snout above the surface of the ocean feel? One day the mosquito becomes a mosquito: it stands upon the water on fragile bent legs slimmer than the taut line of the surface itself. And when it releases the hooks of its feet from the water, it floats straight up, as if gravity were in the sky.

Have you ever really watched a mosquito, as if it, too, could be beautiful? Have you seen it lift and fall like filtered light, bouncing on columns of air with the rhythm of water in its flight—a flight that is more like tracing stillness than moving? Have you seen it, really—thin and quavering, sharp as a pin?

Is anything simpler? Is anything better camouflaged than this creature which looks like an indentation in a leaf, or a scratch, or an imperfection in your vision?

It is of imperfections that the whole world is made.

In a universe so rich and solid and laden with color, the mosquito is a ghost—weightless and frail. Since it escapes danger by nothing but luck, since it is vulnerable to everything, it has no cause to fear any other being. If anything, it must fear vaguer things, like the wind.

It has no blood of its own. It is so small, so meaningless. It is not even real. It lusts for the lifeblood it lacks—it is a tiny wisp of emptiness; it is hunger itself.

Its prey is not a single being—nothing so large could be recognizable to it—but rather heat, moisture, breath and blood.

Its prey is life itself.

Only a female mosquito drinks blood. A male prefers flowers. But a female sleeps in some pocket of a tree's bark, her body heavy with blood, and nourished by that blood she creates her eggs. And when she finds that perfect still dampness somewhere in the forest, she dances her eggs onto the surface of the water.

And new generations of mosquitoes are created through human blood. Does that tiny mosquito spirit dream strange, incomprehensible dreams of human suffering while she sleeps in her tree, dreaming up her children? Do her children carry along the air some thread of human longing—that special kind of thirst that can never, ever be quenched?

They trail like ghosts along the air, stealing from the lives of others, using their thirst for blood to create new life.

And in the summer the lively, abundant, glorious forest is webbed with the whine of a million mosquitoes.

It seems a tormented sound to me, like suffering made into song.

Alone in my cabin that summer, I began to write again, though it wasn't the writing I'd come there to do.

Desire was like a silky mucous in my heart.

The feeling of writing was white and slow.

And the mucous dried in the wind of my aloneness to a steely fiber, and the fingers of the words stretched it and rolled it into a silver thread.

Evenly and with splendor, like some gleaming dream.

I wrote of the boy and me, and the dance we danced, without touching. Sometimes the story was the most important thing. More important, even, than the stuff from which the story was made.

Maybe that was why I couldn't get out of it.

And yet maybe it finally became a story because I knew it would end.

FALL

~

Colors are the wounds of light.

-William Blake

Nine

"There's a cat under your cabin," said the boy casually, standing in my doorway.

I ran outside, stooped by the steps and peered under.

She was black, small, folded and trembling. Eyes and nose pointed forward. Aware and unaware of her power at the same time. She would neither come nor run away.

The boy hesitated beside me. I could see his boots near my face as I waited there, crouched into a bundle myself, wanting to call to her but ashamed of my eagerness. He stood wary and still, watching me watch the cat.

"Where did it come from?" I asked pointlessly.

"I don't know," he said. "Tell it it's in a designated wilderness area, and it's not allowed here."

"Why is it my responsibility?"

"I don't know. You're the one who likes cute furry things."

When had I ever said that?

Only after he went away did I think to wonder why he'd come.

Taking my time, I coaxed her out. It was comforting to meet an animal that knew what people were. Her tiny face tapped the air just around my fingertips—question, question. She tiptoed in the negative space around my body, nudging the air, like an edge of water lapping at the shore. When she stood still, energy seemed to flip up and down her body like quick smoke.

Her elbows were perfectly angled, her tiny white chin perfectly locked. She made everything around her seem sudden and clumsy.

I didn't have to see her from behind to know that she was female. I sat in the dirt and let her come around me, gentle as a mist, and lost my thoughts in the details of her motions.

It was so easy to make her love me. It happened in days.

I knew she wasn't supposed to be there, but nobody seemed to care that much. I was the strange one who spent more time with animals than with people. They left me and my cat alone.

The boy kept threatening to take her away—to drown her in the lake or something. But I knew he wouldn't really do it.

I saved scraps of meat from the dining hall and fed her on my doorstep. And then I let her in. And then one day she just climbed self-assuredly into my lap and melted there while I was writing.

She began to follow me around the cabin, asking to be touched.

All through the summer, I wandered the same forest the boy wandered, alone in my aloneness as he walked alone in his. I wished I knew the terrain of his landscape, the design of his perception, the language that footprints and scents spoke to him. I ached to know the secrets of his spirit, the direction of its thrust, the location of its heart. Did it long to be loved, as I did, by this wild, wordless world?

As the light once exploded and shivered upon the flanks of snow drifts in ever-shifting rainbows, now it flurried like dust into the weightless shadows and sun ghosts of a forest summer. And it opened and closed like eyes all over the lake, dazzling in the distance and pulsing softly up close. And ants poured from a rotting stump, in patterns.

If I watched in a certain curious and desireless way, I could see how the patterns were born and born again in everything.

The wind, the light, the water, the ants. The wind blowing the leaves that flickered the light. The light on the water. The ants like sparkles of light, never still.

Everything expanding and contracting, pushing and pulling, gripping and releasing. Winter and summer, female and male.

If I watched long enough, I knew that anything was possible. I knew that nothing had to be the way it was—that anything could be different. And I thought that in the babbling images of those patterns, that light, I would find the answer—the shift a human being could make in her interaction with another human being that would make everything fall into place.

But now the more I contemplated, the more I felt lost. The more I stared into the water, the more my mind wandered. And as I stared at the torrents of the ants I felt itchy and restless, and my body ached to stand up and move.

Sometimes the girl forgets to be inside her body, with her body touching the cat's. Her hands become dull and distant then, but the cat forgives her this.

Sometimes the girl seizes the cat a little possessively with her hand as she strokes her, and the cat twitches away, but forgives her.

Sometimes the girl is clumsy with surprising noises, but the cat forgives her this, because there is love in the girl, though the love is afraid.

The cat knows about love. Love is what she feels for the grass blade that she nibbles now, and for the pleasingly soft contour of the leg that is familiar to her as she winds around it, and for the soft bark of the stump she knows with her claws, and for the bowl her tongue knows, and the food inside it. Love is what she feels for the shape of her own body as she licks her hips, round in her safe space between the wall and the shadow.

The cat has experience with fear, and how in the presence of humans, fear sometimes lives together with love.

The cat is stillness now. She is waiting. Waiting to discover what happens, what motions open in the space around her. She does not need anything to happen, but she is attending to certain things. She feels safe in dappled shadow. She is watching the world, until it asks for her engagement. She is keeping track. When she feels too much excitement at the sight of some frail running thing in the bush, she channels it into her long, twitching tail, and releases it behind her. She will only move when she is ready.

Some part of the girl makes a noise large enough to make the cat look back. The cat is confused by such noises, and their connection to the soft leg, or the licking hand. She hears the voice and looks up at the face of the girl. The girl's eyes are wide open and staring. The cat is a little afraid suddenly, and narrows her eyes to slits, easing the brightness of that stare. When the face turns away, the cat turns back to her watching, keeping one ear tuned to the girl. She settles into herself comfortably, like layers of cushions. The hand licks her back just lightly now, incongruent and sudden, but she feels the girl's soul warmly inside the girl's hands, and a thin purr runs through her own blood like pain and pleasure at once.

There are parts of the girl that are too-swift movements lurching and frightening, and parts with body and parts without, and parts that are too much at once and interrupt the subtle, low-humming river of the cat's world.

But with the parts always comes love. And the cat knows love, and she loves the girl, whatever the girl is somewhere among those parts—who feeds her and licks her with the hands. And because of this the cat quickly forgets her fright, or her irritation, or her confusion. The more the girl loves the cat, the more the parts come together and begin to make sense.

The cat pauses to curve her side against the body of the girl, before walking on. She knows she is important to the girl, because she allows the girl to love her.

Because the girl needs to love, in order to survive.

The lynx girl was watching me.

The first time I noticed it I was hovering, mosquito-like, at the edges of the group.

It was a weekend. The interns were drinking and smoking together. They were good people, really. But their conversations couldn't hold me. I swayed without purpose between pairs of people, each engaged fully in some linear, well-connected dialogue, which I followed for a few moments and then left behind—almost without being aware—to follow the line of another dialogue nearby. I couldn't explain why I never committed to any one conversation. There was just nothing to hold me. It always happened like this. I didn't completely belong anywhere.

Eventually I would find myself even more removed, listening dreamily to random notes of conversation from different sources—half-grown sprouts of meaning here and there, the music of varying, unconscious tones. And then I was not even listening but merely lulled by the curious disharmony of all the sounds, and watching. I watched, distantly, the style and story of each person's gesturing—the language each person's body had developed to express confidence or to cover fear—and I thought them all exquisite, so fine-tuned and real. I envied them. And I tried to draw myself back into one conversation or another, to find my place in that mortal engagement, but I could not commit my mind to it.

And then I hated myself for my own loneliness, and drifted even further. And already now I was getting up to walk away, plotting where I would escape to.

But as I rose, she looked at me. I noticed her look because I was looking at the boy—the last look I realized I always took before leaving, in case at the last moment some miracle should occur, some way I could not yet imagine that he would turn toward me and everything would change.

But instead he was talking to this girl. And she looked away from him for a moment—he did not seem to notice—and looked at me. She did not leave her conversation or miss a single beat of it, but her eyes found time to follow me. Her gaze was at once curious and self-assured, and followed me with a certain continuity, as if she had in fact been watching me for a little while.

When I looked back she did not look away.

Her gaze, for some reason, made me pause. It made questions billow up in my throat—questions I had never asked myself about the choices I was making in each moment.

She was the animal looking back at me, asking me what I was—but she was more than that too.

It was strange. Like I'd taken my invisibility for granted, and then for the first time, unexpectedly, had encountered someone who could see ghosts.

Outside I walked across the still floor of the sunset forest. I felt the familiar longing. I could hear their voices receding. I wondered where I would go now, and what I was trying to prove all the time by walking away.

At my cabin I watched the little cat crouched on the picnic table, engaged in licking her fur. There was such contentment in the steady motion of her tongue around her own body in the golden light. She licked herself round and round, caressing and enfolding herself in her own self-touch, her own self-knowing. She licked herself smooth and soft. She was a magical cat, invisible until her tongue baptized each part of her into reality. She was licking herself into creation.

One morning the cat was gone. She wasn't waiting hungrily on the step. I opened the door and the breezy summer day greeted me like an empty white O.

Just like it was before. Just a forest again. A world of merciless mystery, where a human being must continue to wander alone among the wild things, strange and out of place, unknown by all and unknown to herself, forever.

I went to the boy, who was in the shed with the wild caged things, gathering his teaching materials.

"Did you take the cat away?"

"What?" he said. "I didn't take your stupid cat."

"She's not mine. I just want to know where she is."

"This isn't a place to keep pets. This is a wildlife center."

"Where is she?"

He was taking the snake out of the aquarium for a presentation, but he didn't jokingly ask me to hold it; he didn't look at me.

"Do you know how many songbirds are killed every year by house cats alone? It's irresponsible to keep a house cat outdoors anywhere, let alone a wilderness area."

"But where did you take her?"

"Look, this is an *ecosystem*. Maybe you should attend one of my classes . . ."

"Look at me!" I grabbed his hand and pulled him toward me, but I may have done it just for the sake of touching him. What shamed me was that he knew it, and recoiled as if I had violated him. I had the hideously human feeling, just for a second, that I wanted to own some small part of him. Any part. The tension in his jaw, for example. The slight chronic redness around his eyes, which I felt sure no one ever noticed but me.

"You didn't take her away because of the 'ecosystem,'" I managed to say, even though, as always, I knew he was probably right. "You just did it to hurt me."

"Bullshit," he said, stepping down with three cloth bags full of snakes in his fists. "Everything is not about you."

And he walked out, leaving me helpless in my shiver of emotion.

How could he be so certain, always? Couldn't he see how the little cat was wild, in her own way? She didn't deserve to be locked up wherever he'd put her. It wasn't her fault she'd been created by humanity, and that as a result she did not belong anywhere in nature—did not belong in the place of her ancestry, and was not allowed to follow her most ancient instincts. I knew he was right, but why couldn't he recognize that this dainty, affectionate creature was also as wild as the raptors he didn't want caged—as wild as he?

Why couldn't he ever talk to me?

I sat inside the cove where I knew I would see the loons on their nest.

It was one of the many places I always imagined were mine alone. But I knew they were not. I knew the boy had been everywhere. He knew this forest better than he knew himself. Better, because he did not want to know himself.

I, on the other hand, came out here to find myself, to go deeper inside myself.

So why did I always feel so lost?

Four loons were circling out on the water. Their heads appeared and disappeared in a magical ring. They were dueling for territory. When one went down they all went down. And then there was stillness. And when one came up too early, then its flat body lilted upon the water in fear, because loons attack from beneath the surface. From the depths with their dagger beaks. From a dark, vulnerable place under the heart.

Both the males and the females fight. Round and round and then suddenly gone.

Sometimes they kill each other.

I heard the shed door close and I hoped it was him, but it wasn't.

I could tell by the footsteps, which hesitated, though not as much as I might have expected—because she never came in here.

She stood in the doorway to the rat room where I was cutting up the bodies.

"Hi," she said, and it occurred to me that she'd come for the sole reason of finding me. I lifted my hands from my work, awash in self-consciousness. It was something about her gaze. I couldn't have said, at this point, what color her eyes were. I couldn't look at her directly. I could feel myself trying to turn invisible somehow, and then I was annoyed, because I couldn't. I wanted her to leave. I was busy in my thoughts; I wanted the world to myself.

"I know where he took your cat," she said.

There were so many parts of that sentence that struck me. Her seeing the cat as mine. Her knowing that I worried about the cat. Her knowing something about him. Her knowing that what she knew about him, I did not know.

I shrugged.

"She's okay," she said. "He gave her to one of the employees who lives offsite. I don't know why he didn't just tell you. He can be kind of an ass sometimes."

As if she knew better than I did, the way he could be.

"Oh okay, thanks," was all I could manage.

She didn't go away yet. What did she want? I wanted to be alone with the sorrow that was even now infusing me—the unstoppable realization I was having about the boy I wanted and this girl. I wanted to be alone so I could stop what I was doing and lean against the counter and think and think, for some indefinite moment.

She was looking at my bloody hands.

"I could never do that," she said matter-of-factly.

No, of course not, I thought, with something like contempt.

How could he like her? It didn't make sense. Didn't he want wildness, toughness, someone impervious to emotion? But she was easy and sure, and somehow, he wanted that too. He wanted that in a girl.

"It must be hard," she said. "To kill them, I mean." She looked into the cages for a moment. "They're kind of cute, almost."

I looked at her now, but there didn't seem to be any judgment.

"I mean, in a way you must not really want to kill them, but the birds have to eat. Nature's so cruel, isn't it?"

I scowled, though I didn't mean to. Her words were so simple, so beside the point, and yet so annoyingly to the point, that I didn't know where to begin.

"Yeah, well," I responded stiffly, with some perverse pride, "that's the way it has to be. What I want isn't really important."

She looked at me and smiled, which at once irritated and unnerved me. Somehow her presence alone had the power to shift the entire mood of a conversation.

This is what she said then. She said,

"What do you want?"

And it was so strange, what I felt. It was like she'd just opened up a little space for me.

I was safe inside this space—this momentary square of silence—but I had to stay perfectly still. Anything I said would be amplified. Any way I moved I would hit the sharp edge of some too-long unspoken thing inside me. Anything I did—anything I said—would hurt.

She didn't seem impatient, the way the boy would have been. She said,

"You're a lot like him."

"What?"

She laughed. "I mean, neither of you want to reveal anything."

I stared at her.

Then she laughed again and made a dismissive gesture with her hand, as if self-consciously, which surprised me again.

"Don't worry about it," she said. "I'm sorry to bother you. I just wanted to let you know about the cat."

Here was the understatement of quiet birdsong inside the cathedral of a sunset.

Here was the tapestry of fog upon the moon upon the marsh, and the fading light shining through the glass of my body as I walked back from the shed in early twilight.

The coyotes calling like howling fairies.

The lake swelling like a soul in the dying light.

The intensity of that poem I kept inside my body—the emotion I called beauty, now rising up and burning my throat.

Surely she was not struck through by glory this way. She was so simple. She could not possibly know how beautiful he was.

But she knew more than she was supposed to know.

In all the history of humanity, has anyone ever been able to answer this question: why does beauty hurt?

Is it because it is too big to bear alone? Because it can never truly be put into words (even the writer only skims its surface, sneaks up on it sideways), and therefore we suffer the fear that we will never be able to communicate or share it with anyone?

Or is it because we feel, in its presence—for so fragile an instant—holy? And then in the next moment we must face all the crass and ugly emotion that is human.

I could never be holy like the lake at the foot of the sunset's cathedral.

Because I was jealous, and scared, and ugly, and proud, and wounded by my own love.

Ten

The boy came bursting into the shed one day and dropped an empty cage on the floor.

"The Great Horned Owl escaped."

"What happened?"

"Nothing. I fucked up. He got out."

He must have just finished a presentation. He had a leash in his hand as he barreled around the rooms, opening and slamming drawers. "Where's that owl call tape?" he asked hurriedly, and then found it at the same time.

I stood still. I was imagining the owl, free.

But the boy paused at the door, his body a blip in space, stopping time. He looked at me, like he'd made a mistake, and then looked down.

"You want to come? He likes you better anyway ..."

And my heart, shocked by gratitude, forgot all about freedom.

It was night already. The forest had closed its curtains, and opened its secret doors.

We passed a small cluster of people near the lights of the main building where he had given the presentation.

"How did it happen?" asked the lynx girl.

He stopped long enough to tell her a story about not locking the cage fully, and the owl hurling himself against it, as always, and flying away.

He was smiling now—a boyish, story-telling smile that he wore especially for the lynx girl. He had time for this story—for her.

She said the thing I had not dared to say, for fear of sounding foolish.

"Too bad he can't just stay out there in the woods. That's where he wants to be."

The boy looked back at her fondly.

"He hasn't been wild in so long," he said, "and he can't hunt or even fly very far because he's blind in one eye. He'd be too vulnerable. He'd die."

Vulnerable. Such envy I felt—that he had never given such a word to me.

"You like her, huh?" I said as we walked away, trying to sound casual. In the darkness, where I could hardly see myself, I felt braver.

"You mean do I like her like her? Or do I like her like her like her?" he mocked.

"You know."

"Listen, I'm not having a deep talk right now, okay?"

At the edge of the forest where he'd lost the owl, he played tape-recorded calls.

They sounded so tinny and clumsy, and I thought, we could be saying anything in the owl's language—we were like bumbling tourists stringing words together in a foreign language without knowing anything of its soul.

But to my surprise we heard a call back. I remembered that the owl couldn't travel far because of his blindness. The boy moved forward eagerly, and I was shocked by the harsh rasp of his boots against the ground, the crudeness of his movements in the slow, patterned darkness.

"How do you know it's him?" I whispered, though the question sounded stupid. I couldn't imagine why he'd wanted me to come. I couldn't think of any way to help.

The boy didn't answer, but played the call again. I stayed still, feeling useless.

No matter how far the owl turns his head, there is a space he cannot see. He follows the images over his left shoulder, and all the way behind him, but they keep escaping into a section of nothingness.

This is not new, exactly. But it frightens him in a new way. And it has never really seemed right, that things happen on one side of his body that he cannot be sure of.

He's flown straight over the arch of the sky and landed deep in that infinity of trees, the family he's been longing for forever now. But now he sits still in a high pine, chasing the nothingness with his head, not remembering.

The universe of his dark sight, where he can travel alone and unhindered.

The sounds seeping from beneath the silence.

The pattern of everywhere motion, signaling like a thousand miniature lights.

But he is still not quite remembering the world, even as it unfolds around him. He is still not quite remembering what it is to be an owl.

Silence. The answering calls had stopped. We could see nothing. The boy played the tape recording over and over.

It sounded wrong. An owl would never call so insistently, so desperately.

I looked at the boy and heard myself whisper,

"Let's just stay still for a few minutes. Then try again."

He didn't look at me but he sat down on a stump and lay the tape recorder in his lap. He did what I asked.

He recognizes himself by that sound. That is his own voice coming back to him.

But no: it is another voice, the voice of another owl. He is in someone else's space. Or someone is calling to him. He is confused. Why do the calls not make sense?

He answers back, just once, and listens again.

There is the call, the call he knows. But from which world does he know it?

There was a world where that sound meant solitude and space, and the power of claiming space, in a forest where one's voice was heard and recognized.

But there was a world more recently in which sounds were singular and dull, in which no sound communicated anything. A world in which there was frequent fear, but never any danger, and constant helplessness, but never any great hunger. And in that world he did not have to chase the invisible space over his shoulder, for nothing moved to draw his eye.

He knows that call, but who is calling, and who is he? He has forgotten what owl means. He knows only that the call is familiar. It is safe, yet unsafe. For how long has there been this terrible mixing of safety and fear?

He sees the familiar large beings shaking the trees. He has heard them all along. But there has been so much, so much to hear and see, that he has not been able to focus on them until now. One, like him, does not know what she is. But she is becoming clearer, and he can hear her silence. She is like a newborn animal learning to stand. Once she has a foothold in the pattern of sounds, she just keeps rising, into his invisible ears.

I knew about silence.

Maybe I was wrong and we should keep playing the owl calls. Maybe we should walk around and search. Maybe the boy was sitting there wondering why he'd brought me; or worse, maybe he actually believed me, and then I would end up being wrong.

But beneath the frantic shuffle of self-doubt, behind the caged pacing of my uncertain heart, I felt some flame brighten.

It brightened and softened, experimenting with itself. It lifted its shoulders and opened its eyes. It began to spread its wings.

I realized the boy was behaving strangely, as if he'd forgotten his tracker skills and his forest knowing. He was upset, I realized. He knew he'd messed up.

I knew about silence. It was my language, and it was the owl's too.

They see little, hear little. He can tell. But they frighten him anyway. He will fly away. And again.

The male is frightening because he means to be. He is aggressive and he plummets toward the owl with a clear intention of capture. The owl knows himself when this happens: he is the one who flies away.

But the female is even more frightening. She is as powerful as the male—in fact more so, because she senses more, and has silence inside her. And within silence, he knows, lies patience, and within patience lies inevitability. But she pretends she is weak. She pretends she is something else. She confuses him by holding still, crouching small, turning away. But he sees her hunger fly around her in a blind desperation, out of control. It is unpredictable and large and dangerous. He keeps his focus on this—the hunger surrounding her, and when it moves toward him, he flies away.

He was so close. When the boy played the recording again—hesitantly, unsure of himself—the owl called back from right above me.

When the boy stood up and went toward him, the night was so quiet I felt I could actually hear the sound of the owl flying—that sound which is the absence of sound, the sound of breath extinguished. There was some fascinating horror in that particular silence, like the eerie silence of visions under your eyelids before sleep.

Now we could see him. He stood there on the branch like a creature who didn't know what it was anymore. Each time the boy went toward him, he flew away again, but only to hunker down on another perch nearby. I suddenly imagined how afraid he must be, with his wild intuition dulled from long hours caged, and his injured senses flailing in the abyss of a freedom he had fought for blindly without remembering until now its terrible complexity and danger.

I wanted to tell the boy to stop again for a moment, to let silence fill the emptiness again and cushion the sharp unease between worlds. I stepped as quietly as I could toward him and whispered his name, reaching my fingertips toward his shoulder. But he turned around so fast I stepped back, and then, with an irritated flourish, handed me the glove.

"You want to do it?" he said out loud.

I opened my mouth to protest but he nodded at the glove, already in my hand, and I knew I couldn't give it back.

I turned toward the owl in a panic. I couldn't even really see him anymore. I didn't know what to do.

The wind blew through the pines.

This has happened to him before. There will be a moment where suddenly he understands. What exactly he understands, he does not know. But it is like the understanding he used to feel long ago at the moment when his talons fit perfectly around a warm body thrusting into his grasp, and for a moment he could not tell whether he had captured something or something had captured him. It will be like that now. In a moment something will come forth from her body that wants him, and he will lose himself in that inevitability, and the whole forest will close in upon that moment, just as his talons will close around the round flesh.

For he can see her hunger settle itself inside her body now, and it does not frighten him quite as much—for now that she shows it to him honestly it feels as gentle and weightless as the breath of leaves on a summer night. She does not come suddenly toward him but moves like the movement of trees as they grow, at once determined and surrendered.

He turns once more to look behind him, but the thought of flight confuses him. He feels himself already a part of her movement. Like a wing catching the wind, and the wind lifting the wing, he feels himself already grasping, and grasped.

I looked back at the boy, wanting to say I couldn't do it. But he gestured his hand toward me with that challenging eye, and I knew he would never let me out now.

I won't be able to do it, I thought in a rush, but I'll just make the effort. I won't think; I'll just walk in the owl's direction with my fist raised.

Which I did, and he appeared and flew away.

I looked back at the boy, feeling foolish. But to my surprise, he was looking not at me but in the direction the owl had flown.

I saw the anxiety in his bent stance. I saw the hope in his gaze—the hope that I would save him from the mistake he had made in letting the owl escape.

I saw—how can I explain?—that suddenly it was my responsibility to be brave, to rescue both the owl and him.

I remembered that everything I did had consequence. That the hand I raised in offering to the owl had both caressed and killed.

I didn't know exactly where the owl was but I walked forward, ducked under a branch, looked around. I could feel something bright in my throat—a sort of pure motion, that was neither hesitating nor hurried but absolutely sure.

I don't know what made me turn toward the owl. But when I saw him I was surprised at his small, warm, jagged shape. He looked so human, all alone there in the graceful, invisible infinity.

I walked toward him with my arm raised because I was the only one who could do it, and because I knew that despite all my romantic dreams of freedom he could not survive in the wild after all.

And because of my admiration for the wildness he would always carry in spite of this.

And because of the power that—whether I wanted it or not—I had over him.

Without touching him, I lifted each of the straps that dangled from his ankles, and pressed them with my thumb against the palm of my glove. He clacked his beak, looked away toward freedom, and looked back. He couldn't decide, so I did.

I lifted my wrist and he stepped onto it: one, two.

That was what really happened. It happened because there was no other choice. It was the only thing that could happen.

I felt the thump of satisfaction in my heart, and the ripples of sorrow around it.

I had never had to prove anything to the raptors. They knew my humanness already. It was I who had never been able to admit to it—who had stumbled over it like something not part of me, frightening them away with my own fear.

The boy was ready behind me with the cage. He opened it, concentrating on the owl, as if not at all surprised by my feat. When I maneuvered my arm toward it, the owl began to flap around in a terror.

"Sh-sh-sh," murmured the boy to the owl, so gently it broke my heart.

"Good job catching the owl," the lynx girl said to me in her simple way. She said what the boy could not say. She said what neither of us could say.

She had approached me as I sat on top of the picnic table outside my cabin in the morning, my feet on the bench, writing something down. I could tell she was curious. I could tell, even, that I wanted her to be curious, but I put the notebook aside and pretended it wasn't there.

Then the boy, passing, came over too, and I knew he was there to see her, so I looked away and clung to my loneliness.

They talked for a moment, and then she walked away, but he stayed. He sat down beside me. I was elated. For a moment I thought, all I have to do is stay still, and they will come to me.

He smiled at me in a friendly way, like everything had always been this easy.

"How are you?" he said, like he meant it.

"Okay," I said, because I never know how to answer that question.

He looked away, nodded. What did he want? Was there something more that he wanted?

I was thinking about this very hard, gazing at the pretty lynx girl as she walked her particular, human walk away down the trail, when I heard him say,

"I kissed her."

I looked at him. His face was a whole new picture somehow. His smile was crooked and embarrassed, and his eyes looked like water. Frantically I replayed the conversation they had just had beside me, at high speed, searching it as if I could be comforted by some cue that I had already known this. I wanted not to be surprised.

But my mind failed me. I just imagined him leaning toward her face.

I felt nothing. Later, much later, I would find a place to feel what I would have to feel. I would find some distant wash of marsh, some stand of bare, crow-pecked trees, some haven of lonely, animal-warm grasses, and curl up in the shelter of the wind . . .

For now I only said, in a voice that barely escaped me,

"So what's happening between you?"

"I don't know. I'm afraid she won't like me. People will tell her what an asshole I am."

So for her, he did not want to be that way.

It was not that he could not be in a relationship. It was that he could not be in one with me.

Things like this, you realize without really thinking them. They are events that happen inside you, and continue to happen inside you, a long time later.

But I said, "Why do you always say you're an asshole?"

I expected daggers, but I got silence. He had something he could not say.

I treasured this. The truth was that no one knew this silence but me. He would not have given it to anyone else—not even the girl. I realized I had what he needed. I was the keeper of beauty. I had saved all the moments that he didn't know enough to keep. I had drawers and drawers of his beauty, preserved and filed away. But if he saw all that, I now knew, he would be afraid.

So I only said, "She doesn't think you're an asshole. She likes you."

He looked at me.

"You think so?"

Then he laughed. Even then, he had revealed too much. He felt naked, and grabbed at something with which to cover himself.

"Is this the deep talk you want to have with me? Is this deep enough for you?"

"I . . ." There were so many conversations I'd had with him in my mind, so much I had imagined saying. I wanted to tell him that he knew me, really. He knew all my weaknesses.

"So what about you?" he said. "You like anyone here?"

"I don't know," I said foolishly, "I mean . . . it's just that . . ." I saw a white wall in front of me. There was the silence of my love for him, and no way around it. There was the meaninglessness, implied by his question, of every intimacy we had shared.

He laughed at me then, finally, as I'd been waiting for him to do. I almost felt relief in the pain of it. Like the strange relief I felt when the deer slipped into the trees and was gone, or even, sometimes, on the nights I lay awake waiting for the boy and he never came.

"What?" he said. "Fucking express yourself, for god's sake."

"I'm just . . . . I'm different. I mean, you don't understand," I said, but it sounded old.

"No, I don't understand," he said. "I can't seem to have a normal conversation with you."

And I was being still like the mouse trapped beneath the snow, but I realized the snow had melted. I could no longer pretend I was the sole proprietor of loneliness. He, too, wanted more than I had ever been able to give him.

"Never mind," he said, and then, as if he might just as easily never have mentioned it, "Actually, I'm leaving soon."

"What?"

"I got a position with those loon conservation people up north. It starts in two weeks."

I could hear my own breath as it left me. I tried to think of something casual and appropriate to say, but I kept looking at the same wall. How had it come to this? I was the one who did not belong to any people, anywhere. Shouldn't I have been the one to leave first?

"So you'll finally have some peace around here," he said, smiling quietly and not looking at me.

I wanted to think about the softness of that smile. I wanted to think about the apology implied in that statement. I wanted to think about the emotion I felt in the space between our faces, and the fragile state of tension that his distance kept it in.

But I was lost in the future, in a forest where he no longer lived. A forest where, for three, inexplicably essential seasons of my life, my desire for him had been the only story I could find.

It was almost autumn.

I sat by the lake while the two of them went to capture the loons together.

I had heard him telling her about them. They can't actually walk on land, and it is a great effort for them even to fly. They spend their whole lives in the water.

I stayed there and watched for the loons all through the end of the day, and throughout the sunset.

I waited a long time before I began to see them. They were there all along, their slim heads like curls of ink rising and falling. Their silhouettes were hardly more than a ripple in the breeze. They did not mean to be seen.

The first shade of evening came.

The water jostled the light about, making images of the seams of a face, laughing, and now collapsing. Memories, was all.

In the foreground, ducks with slippery red-maned heads, like feathered salamanders, dove delicately in and out of the water, dashing now across the surface in cold splashes of fear. I wished the boy were there to tell me what they were—so sleek, like little women.

And there were the mallards (I knew them), like water deer, easing in and out of the reeds, casual and rhythmic. There were herons lurking near me, with eyes like arrows, focusing with insect brutality on their prey, expertly guiding the tension of hunger with each step. I had heard them sometimes in the morning fog, snorting like bulls and coughing like gruff men from the tangled trees.

I knew this place. I knew it like a home.

In the second shade of evening the sky began to waken, brighter than day. There was a diamond blue, too perfect, like the eyes of the dying. The water lay imageless now. It rolled lip upon lip to my shore with an unyielding softness, a constant silver, so silent it seemed to enter right up into me.

He had been so proud when he saw the first loons. He said he had sought their nest for an hour, and stalked them until he saw where they went. But had he watched them like this, for hours in one place? Had he watched them perfectly still on their nest, both male and female taking turns guarding it all the way into the black round blue of near-night?

Had he seen them during the day sometimes, how their beaks hung open like scissors and their necks swayed like snakes in the dizzying charm of the heat?

How they panted, flopped like seals back down to the water. How they gazed at each other sideways from their red eyes.

Their black heads, slinky with water, appearing again and again in the magnificent distance. And their cry now, which was to me the voice of longing, if longing had a voice.

Loons live their whole lives in the folds of that changing, nameless darkness: water.

They can hardly even fly.

How I longed for him to sit down beside me at the edge of the lake tonight, as the fever of the sunset passed, and help me bear the weight of beauty.

To know, with me, that the loon has three songs, one for each shade of evening.

The first was a simple shot of sad silver, arching over the wings of the setting sun. This was the song they used to call each other home.

The second was a fiery knife hurled bouncing into the sky, slicing it again and again to bleed that unearthly light. That was what the male sang when he was angry.

The third song, the tremolo, was like the sound of water—but glowing, as if with fear. It reminded me of those myths where the hero opens the secret, sacred thing the gods gave him, before he is meant to, and the spirits fly out in a terrifying nakedness and overwhelm the world. The sound of a soul broken into before its time.

I wished the boy could hear the loons with me—just before the veil of light fell, finally, away from the stars.

But I would walk back alone long afterward, and be frightened in the dark, and pass by his lone yurt and glance over, and be amazed by how deeply it moved me, just to imagine him sleeping.

~

The world was a series of concentric circles.

There was the ragged sound of my shoes against the leaves—singular, round explosions in space. Surrounding this: the cold, open darkness.

The roundness of darkness is contained somewhere in its presence—that silent opening to nothingness that is comfort and loss at once. The abyss is round.

And surrounding the darkness was the ring of this knowing—ominously beautiful—that somewhere inside the darkness, inside a warm room, two bodies entwined each other in that thoughtless, private freedom of flesh, and neither was mine.

Had they made love yet? With what patterns of touch had they conjured each others' passions? With what words? With what shapes of lips, with what softening of eyes, with what sudden longing and sudden giving in?

The first time I'd made love to that boy, I'd laughed inside at his childish game of charm and seduction. But now all I could remember, as I imagined their faces leaning closer and closer together, was the glimpse I had gotten of his heart. I felt sure now that I remembered it—that sweet wisp of uncertainty inside him, of not knowing, of wanting to do it right, of not wanting to be hurt.

And that hunger inside him that, swamped so deep in my own hunger, I had never really opened to—never really seen.

She now, in her simplicity, would take it readily in her hands, on her tongue—never knowing how hard I had tried. I knew that she would.

The darkness breathed, and sighed, and was empty. The dense meaning of trees dissolved into paper. The wind was still. I could not feel my feet. I was a mosquito, I was nothing.

But there came a sound, from behind the cabin I was passing. A sound that made me real again. A sound that made me feel, for a moment, complete.

She was alone in the moonlight, her shape surprising and unnameable, like the owl when he forgot what he was in the wild that night.

There was a sound like loons and weeping. Her voice, deeper than I had known, made my body stick to the ground and my heart sweat from my face. It emptied me and filled me, emptied me and filled me, repeatedly and at the same time.

This lynx girl, not sleeping with the boy tonight after all, but choosing her own space alone in the moonlight, was playing a guitar and singing some sweet song I never knew—crystallized by the beauty of not knowing that anyone could see her.

I stared at her body, and the movement her voice made in her, as she sat hunched over in the half-shadow of the cabin wall.

I knew what her aloneness felt like.

I knew what it felt like to spin a holy space of aloneness like that and try out a song, a story piece by piece, feeling gradually more confident as the path of one's own self began to look more promising, and hoping the trees were listening and that somewhere some god would understand.

I could never have imagined this. She seemed more like me than I had ever guessed, and that made everything worse, and everything better. It made the thought of the boy smaller, and my loss of him greater.

Beauty is the feeling of pain and joy at exactly the same time.

She was going to look up and see me. I spun away and moved past the cabin. I felt so sad and so grateful. I didn't know anything. I didn't know what I was.

Eleven

In midsummer, the first mammals had begun to arrive at the rehab center. They usually stayed for only a short time, before we shipped them on to a bigger facility, because we did not have the resources to do large-scale rehabilitation in baby season.

We received baby squirrels, feeble and pink, like gregarious little rats with character and infantile passion. We received a box of complaining baby raccoons, who wailed and tossed in the T-shirt cloth and wouldn't suck at their bottles, and who all died before they had ever opened their eyes. We got an adult male opossum, scrawny and stinking and always hungry, who snuffed contentedly through his day-long supply of fruit and meat and mush, and who would stay with us for a couple of months.

Mammals—hot and earthbound and intimate.

One day, later in the summer than was normal, we got a fawn.

He was small enough to carry in my arms. He could barely lift his head, he was so weak from being fed cow's milk for days by the family who had rescued him. I held him steady with one hand while I fed him formula, for the two days that I was allowed to do this, before he was shipped to a better facility that would try to save him.

His fur was rough, the fur of a wild thing. Not much different than the opossum's fur, or the squirrels'. His body was warm like a person's body. His face was bony and complicated, with almost too much contour—like an adult's developed expression forced into the face of a baby. I couldn't believe how much longing and hunger could cry out of that small face. I couldn't believe how still he kept just to feel the touch of my hand, snorting tiny, self-comforting breaths, like a baby dragon.

The lynx girl had come in quietly and asked if she could help with the evening feeding. She seemed overcome.

"Oh my God, he's so beautiful. He's so beautiful," she kept saying. But she spoke very softly, and didn't shine her face directly toward me like she had done before. There was something hidden about her today.

Afterwards we walked outside together. I was shaking a little.

"Thanks for letting me help," she said, and it sounded like she was just being polite. I looked at her.

"What's wrong?" I said. I was scared. Maybe I was interpreting her incorrectly.

But when I said it she stopped walking. She looked at me with the smile I knew, but her eyes held the echoes of tears.

"Just . . . goodbyes are difficult," she said. And I thought, of course, the boy was leaving in a few days, and she had no reason to pretend, like I did, that it wasn't happening—that she didn't care.

"I'm sorry." To my surprise I felt stung by compassion. And she seemed to know it somehow because as we kept walking, slowly, she put her arm around me—with complete comfort, as if we had done it so many times before—and said,

"Thanks. You must wonder why I'll miss him. You must think he's a jerk. I see the way he treats you—he's so cold to you sometimes, I don't get it. I've asked him about it, and he won't tell me why."

I didn't know what to feel when she said that. I could see her out of the corner of my eye. I concentrated on the pattern of rust-earthen freckles: constellations on her skin. There was something so intimate in looking at them—like a quicksand of warmth. I had to look away now, embarrassed.

My heart felt hot and I wanted to ask her questions but I didn't know what they would be. And I felt weak with the experience of feeding the fawn. And maybe I liked this girl, after all. And I didn't know whether I should put my arm around her too, but it seemed the appropriate thing to do, and then after I did I felt stiff and confused, not knowing when I should take it away—not wanting her to feel overburdened by my arm or invaded in some way. My body was a formless, hungry flame I didn't want her to know about.

But through the mossy piles of her hair, I felt her spine like a row of magical, feverish stones. Her hair trailed down her back like ivy. No matter which way she turned, she was always beautiful, because her beauty was certain and uncomplicated. She was beautiful the way a mountain is beautiful: there is no color or curve, no way it turns the light, no softening that shapes it over time, and no shadow it casts that would somehow be ugly—that would make it look dull or disproportionate or insincere.

A handmade body, sturdy, and tougher than I'd realized.

At the fork in the trail where we would part, we stopped. I stared at her eyes, amazed at the way their simplicity turned to pain like that. It was a pain I'd never earned—pure and blue. It had a clear reason, and it lived because of that reason, and when one day that reason faded—when she forgot him, one day—the pain would fade and the eyes would be bright and new again.

This was not the immortal pain that I tended and nourished in the privacy of my shadow. My pain flourished in the absences of things, in the negative space of constant longing.

It would be fantastic to be able to cry that way, with the tears helplessly tracing the bones of the face, nestling between the lips. I had always wanted a face like that, effortlessly feeling.

It wasn't the boy I wanted then. It was her love for him. The tangible, requited, sensible truth of her real-life love—a love I'd been singing about in my heart without ever saying it aloud, a love I'd been longing for without ever having proof of it.

I didn't know what I was. I didn't know what to say. She smiled at me and tossed the tears aside.

"Hey, let's go for a night walk," she said. "Do you want to?"

I am the one who carries beauty. I am the one who bears this weight. I am the immortal who traces like a fairy the hot flesh of life, spinning a single drop of its blood into poetry. Beauty is my god, my reason, my sacrifice.

But what is beauty? Is it the animal herself, and the way she curves her ears innocently forward to catch my voice? Or is it me watching her—her image in my eyes? Or is it the longing I feel in the face of this moment, knowing that no one but I has ever witnessed it?

This longing for my own seeing—my own love—to be seen.

*If only I had a voice like the loons on the brink of night. If only
a human voice could have the subtlety of the wind.*

*If only the boy could hear my silence, the way I heard his con-
stantly—day and night and even in my dreams.*

I couldn't ask her anything about him. I couldn't bear it.
Instead I said to her,

"I have a secret."

She looked at me smiling, like secrets were easy.

"What?" she said.

"When I was little," I said, "I used to wish I were a deer. I
used to dream I would just magically turn into this animal,
and everyone would be amazed, because they would see me for
what I really was."

I laughed, afraid.

She said nothing, but her silence was the same temperature
as my body. We began walking in the dark. She took my arm.

"Or sometimes," I continued, "I imagined a deer would
come up to me in the forest, and she wouldn't run away. She
would come through the ferns to where I stood and put her
face in my hand. She would come and walk beside me—she
would always walk beside me, like we were part of each other. I
just . . . They're my favorite animal—deer . . ."

I turned to face her and she faced me back, and raised her
eyebrows, waiting.

"I still wish that," I said desperately. "I feel like I don't belong
in this world, sometimes."

I felt foolish now, just as I'd suspected I would. All the

romance left me at the sound of my own voice. What was I say-ing? Why did I wander so hungrily along those animal path-ways, longing to see them? What did I want?

Perhaps I'd made it all up. Everything. Everything I'd ever thought I'd felt—maybe it wasn't even real. Because I wasn't real. Because I only loved other things, while I myself was nothing.

A mosquito.

An immortal with no voice and no right to emotion.

And because she and I, if we spoke now, were only clumsy humans at the foot of beauty. This is what happened, when one spoke the truth aloud.

"Why do you love deer so much?" she said.

And I wanted to say, "I can't explain."

I wanted to say, "You wouldn't understand."

I wanted to turn her attention away from me and ask some question like all those questions I'd asked the boy, like "What do you love?"—as if by digging deep enough inside him, I could somehow make him speak aloud that which I never dared speak, as if somewhere inside him I could find an image of myself that I could bear.

But of course, he had only ever been able to express himself. And the girl, now, would only be able to express herself. And I . . .

I knew that my love for the animal was real.

"Because their silence makes them strong," I said. "They're so quiet, and gentle, and soft, and graceful, and you hardly ever see them. But that's what makes them strong. That's what helps them survive. And they know exactly where they fit in. They move through the woods and the woods just opens to them, they just blend in, like they're a part of everything."

She smiled. "Oh," she said, "like you."

I looked around, confused. She didn't understand. The for-est looked like a fantasy right now: moonlight bled between the oaks like strokes of madness, like the howling of coyotes, like the footsteps of dreams. Nobody could see this but me. Nobody. I was sure of it.

"No," I said emphatically. "No, you don't understand. It's like the way I wish I could be."

She took my hands in her hands, and took my eyes in her eyes, and I found that being seen was much easier, much more painless, than I'd thought.

"It is the way you are," she said. "Everything you love . . . is the way you already are. That's why you know how to love it."

And I realized that all this time, after all this longing, it was I who was beautiful.

Our hands made love first. Hands over slim freckled arms, shivering up against each other, brushing dryly, unwound. Like the restful sigh of the yellow winter grasses. Like a slow wandering through twilit gardens, cold moon-wet leaves, where shapes are frayed in the darkness and breeze, between uncivil earth and tearful stars.

I thought briefly of crimson flowers. But I thought nothing else.

She said, kissing me with lips like sleeves of cool water,

"I think you're so soft and pretty."

Like I was the feminine one. With my unshaven legs, my feet red and calloused from walking barefoot in the forest, my bony knees, my dirty fingernails.

I couldn't believe there was another body in the world like mine. Like mine, and not like mine. Rounder breasts, like earthen mounds, rather than pointed like waves. Sturdier hips, a softer belly. But a body that sighed like mine—that yielded, like mine, to long butterfly strokes. I knew exactly what it wanted. I felt the roads of desire on her skin where a man would be lost.

I was overcome with empathy. I felt my body and her body and the whole glorious forest, all at the same time, and I knew how it all fit together. When she touched me I felt no lust, but like I would shatter into petals of light.

Later we sprawled on the earth and I felt the surprising reality of dirt. I had thought she was too simple, too easy, too peaceful for beauty. Now she lay like wilderness before me, her body asking my mind to start again.

I realized I'd never had any special reason for being alone in the world. That was the part I'd made up.

And that night she planted me in the earth, and I started to grow.

In the old Celtic stories, the deer came to lead the people into the Other World. Into the gateway between day and night, the time when deer are awake and moving. Into a flickering space of twilight where the colors have already fallen but the darkness has not yet risen, and the leaves shine white and absurd, glowing upon the vision, as if anything could happen.

The deer would lead the people into the darkness, into the earth, into the reflection of the world. Into a world timeless the way beauty is timeless—where people lost time, lost whole lifetimes. Into a reflected world, the dream of the world before it comes. The fantasy of the world, the poet's fantasy, which is a world in itself—without the flush and touch of life but full of wonder.

The Other World is never the same as reality—the way life actually happens. But it is both fueled and answered by life never the less.

Right in between, where the deer walk, between dusk and dawn, between sleep and waking, I had a dream that was like a vision.

I dreamed I was standing before him, and behind him lay a cliff overlooking nowhere, or perhaps the sky. I dreamed of the arc—it could have been a rainbow—that passed between us, through the spoken realm above and the unspoken realm below, conscious and unconscious, so that we were merely two points on a circle.

I dreamed he already knew me. That everything I could say to him he already knew.

That everything I wanted I already had.

Twelve

There was a peace now, between the boy and me.

I didn't realize until later that it all became easier once I knew he was leaving. It became easier for both of us. Sometimes we would smile at each other in a wry, soft way, as if sharing some sad private joke that brought us closer.

But though I tried to act casual the day before he left, there must have been something else in my voice that I could not rein in.

I said to him, "Will you go for a walk with me . . .?" and trailed off because I could not say aloud yet the reason.

"Why?" he asked suspiciously. But the way he looked at me, with only one eyebrow raised, made me laugh, and he laughed too.

"Oh come on," I said, "I want to talk to you."

"Uh uh, no," he said, like he knew. "I'm not going."

He was standing in the eagle's cage with the hose in his hand, and he'd finished cleaning the cage but the steam was still rising innocently around him as we spoke, and I could see the life pumping through his body; I could see the transience of his motions; I could see the shape-shifting creature that was his soul.

I couldn't believe I'd actually found him alone—and I knew neither of us had anywhere to go at exactly this moment—and this had to happen. I could feel the universe like a tidal wave moving me forward from this moment to the next.

"Please," I said.

And he looked away, as if pained by something.

"I was just kidding," he said. "Yeah . . . . Just give me a minute."

And now we were walking. Reality was looking stranger and stranger the closer I got to it. Would I really tell him? Was any of this real? Was this whole story a fiction? This boy didn't read fiction. He read bird guides and tracking manuals.

He walked in his usual way, with confidence, as if this were his idea, as if he knew exactly what was happening.

"Hear that?" he said, "Did you hear the loon?" But I heard only my own mind.

Goodbyes mean nothing to him, I thought. *Today is a day like any other for him.*

I thought I could say nothing yet. I had to wait until we arrived at the right spot—until then I would have no voice. I was preparing.

"Do you know where you're going to go after this?" he said conversationally.

"Uh, no," I said. "Maybe west."

"You could be a teacher . . . . It sounded like you did well that day, the day you took the kids to see the foxes."

"Um . . ."

"You'll have to write to me."

"Okay."

"Nah, you won't. You won't write."

I felt so lost. What was he saying? Did he care like this? I wished he would start talking about bird calls again, and be the boy I thought I knew: the one who never looked directly at me, whom I had to stalk sideways. I knew him that way. I knew him by his walls.

But now he stopped at a fork in the trail and said to me, with kindness, with curiosity,

"Where should we go now?"

I thought we would go to the beaver lodge, and I would honor him that way. But I couldn't find it. I didn't know where I was. All I could find, again and again, was his presence beside me, like the dead end in some trickster's maze.

I would die now. I would die. I would just stop here and tell him. I had nothing to lose—not because I was immortal, but because I was mortal.

Mosquitoes and light and air floated around us—a soup of sensation. The matted ground whistled with the memories of life, breeze and leaves and dissolving breath. Silk caught the sun as the fly entered the tapestry of the spider, writhed in her embrace, and destroyed the artwork of the dream so that her hunger could at last be filled.

When the lynx girl had touched me, it seemed like every part of my body had its own soul. When she touched my arms, I felt the ache of ungiven love. When she kissed my belly I felt the peace of eternity. When she cupped my face in her hand, I felt compassion for the hunger of the flesh. When she fingered my hips I felt a tenderness and a sorrow for the long road of longing. When she held my feet in her palms, I felt the strength of my endurance.

Now all the parts of me were mixed up in an agony of anticipation. The thoughts I thought made my stomach hurt and fear wiggle in my throat like the fish in the eagle's beak.

But I paid attention to these things—to my body—so I would know I was real.

I don't want anything from you, I would say.

You don't have to be anything different than what you are when you walk here alone, unwatched and free. You don't have to love me.

I only ask you to listen to me one time.

I only ask you to allow this—this that I feel.

I laughed at him in my mind, as I imagined challenging him.

Would you be able to handle it if I told you I got attached after all? That I broke all the rules?

When I come to you, what are you most afraid of?

Well it is true.

But who can face his own beauty and live?

I will always remember the look on his face when I was about to say everything.

Except that I will never remember it, because I have passed it through my mind so many times that I no longer know what it really looked like. Maybe it was a look of fear. Maybe of uncertainty. Maybe tenderness, or irritation.

I was about to say everything, but I was embarrassed, and

I laughed first. I couldn't help it. Maybe if I hadn't laughed, everything would have been different.

But I don't think so. Real love, I have learned, is not a single moment of perfection, but a long winding road which, in this moment in the forest with the boy I never truly knew, I had not yet even begun.

I laughed. "Hey," I said, and I said his name.

He smiled a smile I did not know, and closed his eyes, so that I noticed as if for the first time the subtleties of his face, the expressions that just barely moved there like water under the ice.

"Shh," he said, and then, quietly: "Don't. Don't tell me what you're going to tell me. Okay?"

And, as if to stop the words, he kissed me.

I remember gripping his muscles, my skin tasting his, so that I might no longer be a body but only an experience of his. So that I might finally get enough of him.

What is flesh, so amazing?

His gestures—his own gestures around my body. His eyes pausing to look into mine, his assured grip as if he knew me now—and when he entered me he threw me back inside myself, and dwelling there, I now felt him truly. The wordless pleading of his body pressed and soaked into the layers of mine, and I filled myself deep and full.

Sometimes I was dancing, loving myself—the patterns of his body a stage for my fingers.

And then I would lose all self again and again in that momentary death of the kiss.

And all would be blackness, all the images would shatter,

and behind them was nothing, and I was not I. We could not have said what motivated us; we could not have said what we were.

And then I would emerge for a moment, to look and breathe again, and to find the beauty only sweeter, only purer.

His face above me, lips parted, skin bright, like a child's.

Which is the true gift: the touching or the opening, the giving or the receiving?

The thinking came in loose, helpless strands. *Does he know me, he does—his face, he does. And this moment will be lost, oh god, and this moment, and this.*

Self and other, self and other, self and other.

The things I remember, I did not feel; the things I felt, I do not remember.

Is it possible to at once recognize beauty and experience it? Is it possible to know that you are happy and still be happy?

Is it possible to want and to have at the same time?

He came, with the help of my hand because we did not have a condom. What came out of him sunk slowly into the warm ground. It did not belong to either of us.

He traced me from my chin to my hip, and looked down at me, sad-smiling.

"Look," he said. "I can't give you what you want. You know that."

The wind was cold on my naked body.

He pulled on his pants, and walked away.

For the first time, I noticed the forest around me, and the twilit sky.

But I don't need him. I don't need anyone.

I promised him this a long time ago, when I traded my heart for touch. When I traded my human heart for that animal perfection of touch—of thoughtless union.

It was perfect. It was perfect that way, to be nothing but my body against another—to be taken and carried and dissolved.

And the animal just walks away. It does not know the other. It does not know the past. It does not think. It just melts into the long shadows and is gone.

I do not need anyone.

I do not see the moon rising.

I do not fear the dark, or my mind in the dark—that alone and homeless ghost.

I wouldn't think to follow him. I will go quickly to someplace safe. I will go to the lake and sit by the silent water, where no one can find me, and wait there until the storm I feel coming now has broken. I will just rest there and be still. I will be safe inside my body, in the darkness in there. I will sink down into that dark place, and rest, and be still, and think nothing.

At the edge of my awareness I am aware of my obedient hands returning my clothes to my body, and of their dampness. I am anxious to get to my safe place. There is a terrible thing that I cannot look at right now. I hold it off to one side, up high, away from my face. In a few minutes I will be at the lake—it is just there, where the light is—and I will put the thing down without looking at it, and it will disappear safely into the water or the earth, and I will rest.

I come to the lake. I don't care about the sunset or the color of the water. I sit down and fold my knees against my chest.

But the homeless ghost will not be still. The terrible thing does not sink, but floats greyly to the surface—floats up before me. And the forest which has been my salvation—god, my inspiration and my religion, my poetry and my answer—begins to close in around me.

I want him.
I want him and he does not want me.
I have lost.
I am alone.
I am alone.

How can it be that as the forest darkens, it becomes a cage?
My body—with its tingling, its pleasures, its soreness, its hungers—closes in upon me.
My mind—with its questions and pleadings and denial—closes in upon me.
My heart—with its weather and its long, long winter nights—closes in upon me.
I would do anything now for meadows, for sky, for flight.
I want to get out.

But now comes the terror.
The sunset, somewhere outside of me, is ending.
I will not look.

I hammer at the walls. I hammer and scream at them as they close in, and I will not look back at the dead space in the middle, at the terrible thing there.

The terrible human thing that I am.

No, no, I am not that. I am not.

But stillness waits.

It waits through the tears that don't ever come after all, and through the useless drama of my heart. *I want him, I want no one, I want connection, I want invisibility, I want love, I want freedom.*

Stillness waits patiently until I am tired of trying to climb out of myself on the string of my wants. It waits for me to realize that I can't ever get out. I can't get out of the woman for whom one night of beauty is not enough. I can't get out of the woman who needs the love of another.

And when I finally stop beating at the walls and turn around, and slide to the earth panting and crying, stillness is there waiting. Smiling simply, she offers up a gift: a small darkness glowing.

The gift, the terrible thing—it is loneliness.

Had I not been lonely, always and forever?

Was loneliness not my right, my title, my pride, the only thing that I could count on—and that which elevated me just above the human?

Did I not fall into loneliness, again and again, like a home? Was I not utterly at home there?

No.

I had never been at peace. I had walked in the forest oblivious and lost. I had spun miles of thought between me and the animals, and not been able to touch them—and they not able to know me. And always, always, I had stood just apart from the loneliness that followed me everywhere.

But I could not escape it ever. I could not escape myself.

I had never really looked. I had never turned around and looked at the loneliness that had stalked me all my life like a patient predator.

What was this, then?

On the outside, a knotted storm, a wretched ugliness.

Meaningless flesh, and a fleshless despair. A cry without form. Hands of desperation that grabbed at my guts like starving prisoners through bars and threatened to drag me into hell.

And inside this, like the tender lining inside some pulsing cavity of the body, such a sorrow.

A sorrow beyond the senses, beyond words, beyond helping.

The sorrow of watching the rat's head burst into blood, and the trembling of the boy's hands. The sorrow of another dawn spent lying next to the empty imprint in the sheets. The sorrow of wondering if beauty can only be beautiful from a distance. The sorrow of winter, of my empty cabin with its empty things that no one would love but me. The sorrow of endings. The sorrow of beginning a story whose ending I already knew, but which I lived out anyway because I could not stop it. The sorrow with which I had clothed love, for as long as I could remember, without even knowing why.

The sorrow of not knowing why. The sorrow of the animal, who succumbs helplessly to sex and hunger and death, without choice, without question.

And inside this sorrow, fear.

Where nothing is heard but one's own heartbeat, and nothing is seen but the backside of one's own eyelids, and nothing is felt but the places where one's own skin rubs against itself like a foreign thing.

For a long time I crouched curled up in the night, surrounded by untold numbers of other beings, and yet still feeling alone. The wind stroked the silence fitfully. It tossed inside the silence like a restless fetus that does not yet know its own name.

I still remember now that through the fear I saw, in glimpses, that loneliness was a palace of the most incredible design.

There were glass hallways glinting with diamonds and rooms of deep blue—blue like the color the snow takes in the evening, in which I would never again feel strange or out of place.

And I saw that all this was not loneliness at all, but the house of my soul, for which loneliness had only been a name.

And that inside this house was the sky.

Just like inside the body there is breath. Inside every room of the body, between the smallest particles of matter, there is only space.

And inside the longing, inside the emptiness, was freedom.
And everything.
Everything I needed.

All that happened was that the darkness woke me to a warm
quick fear that I could feel in my blood.

I looked up and the sun had set, trailing all its passions
behind it; the forest had darkened utterly. In the space of several heartbeats I thought of getting lost in the night, of the
unknown lurking in the ice-still water, of being trapped here in
the cold blackness which felt, somehow, too much like death.

The thoughts made little sense but I felt the confidence of
my limbs as fear motivated them into deft motion. I would
simply follow the edge of the lake back to my cabin, though I
didn't know how far away I was.

I walked quickly, clumsy and human, grateful for my skin
which—so bare and vulnerable—could feel everything, and
for my senses which—so tense and afraid—could sense everything, and for my mind which—so useless in the dark—was
still and quiet now.

I knew my way home.
And this was enough.

*Maybe it was I who never let him get close to me. Maybe I kept
him at a distance because the beauty of wanting him was easier
than finding out that he could never satisfy me if I had him. That
he could never meet me in the moonlit forest, or quell the terror of*

living, or understand me out on the empty glorious ice, or catch me
when I fell from a dream in the morning, or hear the whispers I
whispered to the raptors, or see the gentle painful world I moved
through, every day, alone.

Or could he?

Maybe I was afraid because I knew that he could understand
me, after all.
I mean, couldn't anyone, if I let them?

I emerged from the brush into a clearing along the trail, to
the low watery sounds of the lynx girl and the raccoon man
walking and talking together. I saw all around them the grace
of tree limbs in dream light, the unspoken shiver within all
things living and even within the stillness, and the profundity
of the sky. These things I knew, and had always known.

They turned around and saw me, and greeted me, smiling.

"Out for a night hike?" they asked.

"Sort of," I said. "I almost got lost, actually."

"You wouldn't get lost," said the raccoon man. "That forest
knows you."

I looked up at him, startled into a different kind of silence,
for a moment. There was warmth in his face, and he had eyes
like an owl's, but human too.

Then they settled around me comfortably under the trees,
and we walked for a while, and talked.

I don't know where the boy was then. I guess he was out
there, still wandering in his own night. He left early the next
morning and I never saw him again.

My sorrow came in seasons.

In the spring of it, I would think of the loss suddenly with a fresh and simple innocence. I would be sitting on the worn bench he'd straddled long ago when he'd asked me for the first time to go on a walk in the night with him, and I'd feel a pain I could not make sense of. Real tears passed over my cheeks, and then just as quickly were gone.

In the summer of my sorrow, I missed him hotly and at times with a robust anguish—in my heart, in my mouth. I boiled with memories. I really thought sometimes that I had loved him, with a juicy certainty, and loss was a hot-blooded animal that walked beside me as constantly as longing had. I saw his cruelty and I saw the betrayal in the empty mornings, and I discovered anger.

In the autumn of my sorrow, it all turned to poetry. Emotion became true in a silver way, its passion braver and calmer with distance, and nostalgia built up its own eternal kingdom.

In the winter of my sorrow, the beauty dried up and crumbled. I let my shadow lead me. I did not think or want anymore. And I knew that there were ways in which what had happened between us would never really be okay with me.
But that I would be okay.

Thirteen

If I could give you the beauty I know, boy animal-god, I would give you this:

Your eyes which, in the rapture of your story-telling, become birds.

Your hands which, when desire frees them, open.

Your voice which, when the owl turned wild in the silence, did not know itself.

The hungry thrust of your body which, when invited by a woman, surrenders to paroxysms of music.

The dangerous edges of your face in daylight.

The simplicity of your skin in the dark.

The hot shadow under your hair, the moisture on your neck where I kissed you.

Your heart which, when it falls, makes no sound.

I love you.

I stand before a crowd of adolescent children, with a Barred Owl's talons around my wrist. I am grateful for the stillness she keeps, despite the unease she expresses, sometimes, by clacking her beak. While I speak facts about her from my mind, my body adjusts its posture slightly in response to her movements and the level of tension in her grip. I feel myself held responsible to her wildness by the claws that bind my wrist.

"She looks tame," I tell them, "but she's not at all. She's not a pet. She's only sitting still on my wrist because I'm holding her there with the straps."

So many children raise their hands, with the lonely hunger that overcomes a person in the face of the animal—the hunger which they are hardly aware is moving them, and which later in their lives almost all of them will forget.

I choose the dark-haired girl in the back, with her arm only half-raised. Her voice is soft and some of the other children glance back to wonder.

"Did everyone hear what she asked?" I say. "She asked if I feel bad keeping wild animals in cages."

I hear some muffled laughter. I feel the old loneliness rise in my throat. The owl, made of broken flight and hollow bones, weighs almost nothing. But her trust steadies me.

"No," I say to them, "it's such an important question that she asked. It's a question we have to ask." I stop, face to face with myself, afraid. But then I feel the raptor's talons tighten on my wrist and I remember that loneliness is only an excuse.

"It's a question we have to ask because we are compassionate beings. It's our compassion that makes us save the raptors with the blind eyes and broken wings, and compassion that makes a bridge between our world and theirs—so that I can stand here and teach you about them. And it's also compassion that makes us wonder if we're right to keep them. Maybe we should have allowed them their natural deaths, right?"

I look at the girl and see her eyes and her spine strengthen in response, and I know that what is important is that she feels a little more real now. "It's compassion that makes us human," I say. "It's that certain kind of love. I can't answer her question, but I know that it must be asked."

This is one of the memories that I keep to see myself by. After the boy left, I took over some of his classes. And I taught the lynx girl to do some of the work I had learned to do with the animals, because I could tell that she truly loved them— and that is enough.

I went back inside my cabin that night before the boy left forever. I woke there the next morning and considered the sun.

This was my cabin that I knew so well, and that knew me.

Sorrow was familiar, yes.
Sorrow, and the indescribable light.

Have you ever seen the moment where light begins? Have you stood outside at the beginning of the dawn, and seen sight itself become?

Vastness narrows into form. The sky which was the universe becomes the rose glass bowl of the world—a respite from infinity.

In the beginning, there is only this two-dimensional idea of light. There is only this uniform, reptilian light, pencil-drawn and shadowless.
But look again and there is pink in a cloud. The fence post is red suddenly, and yellow hums on the horizon.

The sky suggests colors one by one in their original hues.

Then all at once, and without mercy, the dawn lays flat the images—meaningless and plain.

If you are muddy with sorrows and thoughts, if you are drunk on your own tragedy, maybe you have not seen enough dawns.

Because in the dawn, there is no such thing as love yet. There are no love songs. There is no heartbreak.
But if you rise out of the blue hills in the morning, you can see unicorns of light walking through them. You can see mist suspended like a shaken belief, and everything—everything—reborn.
And peach appears on the lips of clouds like hunger.

Suddenly the flowers can be seen. They are so startling—every detail intact. They give your eyes no rest; they fill your perception.
You see the first shadow—furtive and transparent on the dirt.
Colors cannot be described yet, only seen.
But differentness begins to arise.
Some things know light now, and some know shade, and some know phases in between.

On goes the day into glory.
May your eyes walk delicately, and see the mosquitoes painting the air softly with nothing, and a couple of spider threads making a

violin of light between the leaves, and the fringes of seed sparkling on the grass, knocking against space—so slight that their next incarnation will surely be air.

Always it will be like this. You will see God only out of the corners of your eyes.

You will know that somehow, everything you want is right here, in the particles of light rising like steam from your pillow in the morning, in the moments of silence before you yourself rise, before any feelings are born.

You will know the sun is behind you, and feel its warmth, as you pause to reflect on the grace of your shadow before you.

But you cannot look. You cannot look directly at the sun, at least not for too long, or you will never see light again.

Be like the trees, then, who have no eyes, and yet live on light.
Be content, then, just to live.
For when you open your eyes in the night, they shine.
I have seen them.

When I return to my apartment tonight, I turn the lights on in my room, shaken, remembering where I am, and where I am not. I take from my desk, from my drawer of sacred things, the one letter you ever wrote me.

Its text is no longer than the width of my hand.

How are you? I am going to Costa Rica in two weeks. Life here is good, but I want to move on. I got your letter by the way. I tried writing you a longer letter, but I lost it on a canoe trip. Basically I just wanted to say that actually I admire you too. I think you're a really good person, and I always liked hearing your thoughts about things. I want you to know that. Good luck with everything.

There is not much to read, not much to read into. But I know now that for you, writing anything at all meant something. Who are you, animal boy, whom I have never really known? I know only that you shared a love of the wild alone space with me, and that is a space that can never be shared with anyone, isn't it?

I have been thinking it's time for me to move back to the woods. There are times in life when you have to live in the city or in town, even though it's not what you want, but you can't stay there too long or you start dying inside. You lose your wildness, your love of being alone, your sense of meaning in the universe. I know you wouldn't put it that way, but you would at least understand.

I keep this letter from you, in honor of the girl I was that loved you.

Whoever you were, I know who she is.

I am finally writing the stories I went there for—the stories of animals.

I think I understand them now, and for that I thank you.

And I still think that really, all stories come from these.

When the fawn becomes real, she follows her mother into meadows at dawn. In the meadows the other fawns come with their mothers, and discover that they are not the only ones in the world. But they do not look at each other long, or gaze into each others' eyes and wonder. They have no time for this, in a world where death could come at any instant. Their eyes look out warily from the sides of their faces, and their faces are not capable of expression—only sensing. They sense each other nearby, and they learn simple trust and distrust, and they practice the movements of their bodies.

Days and nights grow out of each other and light is only a measure of danger. In the safer space between the night and the day, when her vulnerable form in the half-light can seem other than it is, the fawn stretches her long neck and eats from different levels of the forest. She grows, and grows older. As a grazing animal, she is constantly hungry, and constantly eating. She is hunger. Hunger drives her at every moment to live and keep living. And yet it is not painful, because it is constantly filled.

She cannot imagine the strange rhythm inside the body of the predator, whose hunger comes upon him all at once and aches in him with urgency, and who then channels all the skills of his being—the quick senses, the claws, the patience, the speed—into a few moments of ambush, to fill the hunger utterly. How strange that in the hours following, he continues to feel filled—to rest in a state of fullness without motivation, where he can lounge about in the sun, and play, and perhaps hover on the brink of contemplation and dreams.

The deer is always hungry, and always being filled. Always searching, always moving.

And she is always afraid.

She is a being born into danger. She could be taken at any time. Her life walks a cliff's edge overlooking death, and can never take *a step away. She is afraid while her hunger moves her, and afraid while her hunger is filled; afraid when she leaves her baby alone and afraid when she moves close to him again. She is afraid while she is sleeping.*

In this way she walks along the pathways of her life, pathways that others in her herd have made before her—the ones toward food and away from danger. She moves among the others because it is useful to do so, but in the scarce and endless winters when hunger turns almost to longing, each doe in the group is alone.

And when she comes to give birth, she is alone. And when she is finally singled out by the predator because she could not recover from the final winter, and the herd—throbbing with fear—runs on without her into sweet disappearance, she is also alone.

She does not think now, only runs. Everything beautiful that she is—the great wide eyes on the sides of her graceful face, her nimble legs, her deep camouflage, her silent feet, her intimate sensitivity to every variation in the forest's floors and walls, and her ability to leap into the air like a dancer over a fallen tree—was made for this purpose.

She is beautiful because she must run from the coyote. She was made beautiful by fear.

And the coyote is made beautiful by his hunger, and by the chase.

She runs past the branches with their new buds and the ground where the spring grass she's been longing for has finally sprouted in the snow. She runs around the safe haven where this morning she slept. She runs past the thicket where she birthed five children. She runs through the dark grove where the herd has sheltered itself for warmth every winter. She runs out into the open.

All together she does not run very far, because she is weak, and this coyote is strong. And now he has others with him, and she is alone.

When she can feel his breath on her cold ankles she spins and fights. She thrashes at him with her sharp and delicate hooves. But the limp she developed after they attacked her years ago, worsened over time by cold and parasites and the fall she took along an embankment this winter, makes her unsteady. And besides, she is old. She is older than she ever knew she could be.

When they bring her down she does not know enough to resist pain, and so it is not very painful. The coyotes embrace her with their paws and their mouths. She realizes with relief that all of the fear is about to be fulfilled. And so all of the fear is about to end.

And what does the animal know, between life and darkness, between death and waking?

Perhaps she feels the tremble in his muscles clamping tight on her body, and sees the frenzied desperation in his eyes, and recognizes that hunger. She can see his eyes, she can see every hair on his body, and she can smell the blood on his breath. Perhaps, engulfed by his woolly reality—never before having been so close to that which she feared all her life—she feels some concept of beauty graze lightly whatever can be called her soul. Perhaps as she feels him surround her, feels him holding tight and panting with his eyes stretched wide—so alive—she wants to give in to him.

She wants to give him something—he who struggles so painfully. She feels that her life is not so much to give up after all. She feels that everything, suddenly, is easy.

Now, finally, she will rest. Now, finally, she will be free.

But from the embrace of the coyote she carries into death a feeling that she never knew in life.

And in a few more lives, she will be human, and call it love.